THE PATTER ANOTHER BLAST

Happy Birthday Dad!
From Stewart

The Patter

Another Blast

Michael Munro

ILLUSTRATIONS BY
JOHN BYRNE

Canongate

First published in Great Britain in 1988
by Canongate Publishing Limited, 17 Jeffrey Street, Edinburgh.

Munro, Michael
The patter, another blast.
1. English language. Glasgow dialect
I. Title
427'.9414'43
ISBN 0-86241-206-4

Typeset by Swains (Glasgow) Ltd, York Street, Glasgow.
Printed and bound by Bell and Bain, Thornliebank, Glasgow.

INTRODUCTION

This book is a sequel to *The Patter* (Glasgow District Libraries, 1985). While the two volumes are intended to be complementary, each can be read on its own and this one contains only previously unused material. The bulk of this consists of words and phrases that were new to me but a fair amount can be described as unintentional omissions from the first book.

The Patter has been successful beyond the imaginings of anyone connected with it. At the time of writing this piece it has sold well over 100,000 copies and demand shows no sign of petering out. It has found a market not only in the Glasgow area but all over Scotland and the rest of Britain. Numbers of copies have gone all over the world, including most of western Europe, the USA, Canada, Australia, New Zealand, Hong Kong, Fiji, Brazil, Malaysia, and Singapore. The book may be consulted in the libraries of the House of Commons and of the University of Hawaii. Extracts were printed in the souvenir programme of the 1988 Jakarta Highland Games.

Why should this slim, unsensational publication have been in such demand? I would suggest that what *The Patter's* popularity demonstrates is that a great many Glasgow people, whether living locally or far from their birthplace are genuinely and enduringly interested in and attached to their native dialect.

Language, of course, is an item of personal luggage that is easy to carry. Wherever you go, it goes, unless you deliberately attempt to leave it behind, and even then it has a way of turning up when your guard is down. Particularly in a foreign country, you can't help but be aware of it every time you open your mouth to speak, whether to be met with incomprehension or delighted recognition. For the homesick it is a concrete link with home. It is the medium for shared humour, remembered songs and poems, catch-phrases, and greetings that will always identify you more truly than any passport photograph. For many people, then, a book of their own language is a relatively rare and welcome thing, a focus for memories, a souvenir of their own past.

One remarkable aspect of the distribution of *The Patter* is that many of the buyers, particularly abroad, have no real connection with Glasgow, yet they still identify with the book. In a way this is no doubt attributable to the fact that Glasgow is one of the two main tourist images of Scotland (the other being the Highlands), but I feel we can still ask what it is about the Glasgow dialect that makes it so strong, so attractive and memorable.

I am no expert on linguistics and the reasons for language development are as much a mystery to me as to any other layman but I would begin with a little geography. Although it may be easily overlooked when strolling through a suburb or inching through the rush hour in Union Street, this city is a port. Opened to the sea by the Firth of Clyde it sits near the western edge of Scotland and looks beyond the near islands to Ireland and America and its dialect bears the centuries-old imprint of the first of these cultures and a later veneer of the other. Like any port it imbibes a little of everything that passes in or out. It is as cosmopolitan as the one-time second city of a world empire has a right to be.

Yet, if you look at a map you will see that if the Firth of Clyde were merely a broad river valley Glasgow would be a midland city, right in the heart of Scotland. This gives Glasgow an enormous hinterland, both Highland and Lowland, from which it can draw resources both material and human and to which it can be a great central source. My point behind all this is that Glasgow has never been insular and that its language has been enriched and vitalised by a uniquely diverse range of influences.

My second strand in this argument is the character of the people. A large proportion of Glasgow's population has always been, of necessity, used to adversity. Poverty, unemployment, substandard housing, and any other brand of deprivation have all marked the collective psyche, but still the people love to laugh, love to make each other laugh. To get anywhere in a city like this (with too many contenders for limited rewards) you have to be smart, inventive, indomitable. Glasgow has a long history of producing intelligent and original minds; the Glasgwegian craftsman was a byword in many industries that have seen their best days. All of these human qualities are reflected in the dialect. It is funny, often highly imaginative, always accurate, often cruel, never long-winded or tiresome. It has an observation or comment on anything and everything. If you have nothing else going for you a witticism or piece of wry fatalistic humour will often get you out of a bad corner, scythe a bigger opponent to the ground, wreak a fierce revenge on someone who thought he was getting away with it, show anyone who cares to notice that although down you are not quite out.

The 1980s have seen something of a resurgence in Glasgow's fortunes and image. The winning of the Garden Festival of 1988 and the designation as European City of Culture for 1990 are the most obvious fruits of this. The city centre is clamorous with new building and long-overdue refurbishment of the fine and not-so-fine in our architecture. Glaswegian artists and writers have both national and international fame; our young musicians are a thread of quality in the skimpy garment of pop music. Talk abounds of a Glasgow Renaissance although wiser heads argue that there was nothing much to be reborn and we are really dealing with a lot of new growth. No matter, Glaswegians have much to be proud of; they can feel good about being from here in a more positive way, no longer just in the sense of 'Glasgow Rules, OK?' that sprang from a contempt for almost everybody else. But it doesn't do to be convinced by your own propaganda. Only a self-deceiver would conclude that all's right with the city, but this is not the place to enumerate Glasgow's shortcomings or complain that not everyone has a share in the new good times. Suffice it to say that we have come far and still have some miles to go.

This is why I can shrug off jibes that my books present an undesirable side of Glasgow, that I propagate the language of the gutter. While I admit that some of what I record is unpleasant and does nothing for the city's image it is there because what I am interested in is the whole picture, the portrait from the life with no blemishes airbrushed away. However, nothing here is included for the sake of being gratuitously offensive. To those who find cause to take offence I would say: you should have seen what *I* chose to leave out. I want to present Glasgow as I find it, with a balance shifting almost daily between the things that I hate in it and those that I love.

In a book like this I can only attempt to pin down as much as I can of the vocabulary of Glasgow's dialect. There is still so much more to it than the nuts and bolts that are its words. Such subtleties as phrasing, emphasis, and tone must escape the net. How could I convey here the depth of menace that can resonate from a simple question like 'What are *you* sayin?' or communicate the irresistible laughter induced by this or that deadpan observation?

Then there is the language of gesture. Glaswegians tend to be great gesticulators, accompanying their words with an entire sub-plot of bodily movements. If you watch people talking out of earshot you can often follow the conversation by virtue of the pantomime that supports the spoken part. A pint will be referred to with a hand half-open as if round a tumbler waggling in front of the speaker's mouth. If someone brings up the subject of a game of snooker his right elbow will crook and swing back and forth as if guiding an imaginary cue through the fingers of his left hand. If the discussion turns to how the Big Man headed in the winner at the game you will see the narrator cock his head, lift his eyebrows and nod towards a figurative goal. You are shown actual events sketched in a few economical motions. A Glaswegian can communicate disbelief simply by touching a forefinger to a lower eyelid while keeping the rest of the face quite immobile. He can crow over another's embarrassment by licking a finger, holding it towards the red face and making a sizzling noise.

Glaswegians love to dramatise their lives and narratives. They will tell a story, relate some relatively trifling event as if it were a play or film with the narrator as star. I think I can best put this over by indulging in a brief example:

'There Ah am, stoatin doon the street, ye know, no botherin ma arse or nothin, when this windae shoots up an this big wummin hings oot an goes "Hey you!" Ah'm lik that. Ah mean, ye could see she wisny too happy. Ah says "Whit is it?" She goes "See if ye see a wee rid-heidit boay roon that coarner, tell um tae get up here fur his tea this minute." Ah goes, "Is that aw? Aye, awright missis." An there wis Ah thinkin she wis goany pap a boatle at us or somethin!' And so on.

Big words are meat and drink to the Glasgow conversationalist. It is as if wee ordinary everyday terms are not sufficiently vivid or impressive. The patter merchant will not say 'drunk' if he can use 'miraculous' or 'paralytic'. Why restrict yourself to saying 'Give that to me' if you have at your disposal 'Ah'll take command a that.'? What we have here is a people who love talk for its own sake and consequently demand a high standard of entertainment value from the one doing the talking. If your patter's like watter you would do better to keep your mouth shut and just listen.

All of these things are essential elements of Glasgow communication that must remain beyond the scope of this book.

If I have learned one thing from the work I have done in writing this second book of Glasgow language it is that I was guilty of rather too much pessimism when I remarked in the introduction of *The Patter* that Glasgow dialect was in danger of disappearing. While it holds true that the pressures and attractions of American and English speech remain strong, the continual evolution of new Glaswegianisms encourages me to believe that there is life in the old tongue yet. In fact, it could be argued that Glasgow speech is spreading in a kind of imperialistic way, at the expense of other dialects of Scots. I would attribute this to the perception of Glasgow language by young people all over Scotland as being attractive, even glamorous (gallus is probably the best word), leading them to adopt turns of phrase or pronunciations heard on television or in contact with citizens. This is not a process I welcome as I would prefer to see a continuing multiplicity of living dialects but it is as pointless to deplore this as it is impossible to prevent it.

I have treated my material in this volume in the same manner as the first, aiming for clarity, avoidance of dictionary terminology and striving for a light and amusing tone in my examples of usage. As before, the body of the book comprises an alphabetical list of words, following by appendices of rhyming slang and phrases and sayings. I have taken the liberty of adding a new appendix entitled 'Cheek' as I felt I could reasonably distinguish a core of material that is used for this particular purpose rather than meaning what it appears to say.

I would reiterate that I am not in the business of teaching anyone How to Speak Glaswegian. As I have said, the language is a form of common identity and although an incomer may pick up its commonest features and understand all of what he hears he will never pass for a native speaker. Something in his accent will give him away. So I'm afraid that to be fluent in The Patter you have to arrange to be born here. By the way, I have learnt that such a dictionary of a particular area rejoices in the academic title of an *idioticon*. I suppose that makes me an *idioticographer*. What it makes my readers I'm sure I don't know, but I wish them an abundance of pleasure or enlightenment or whatever it is they desire from this little book.

Acknowledgements

As with *The Patter*, this book would not exist without my fellow citizens of Glasgow; talking and listening to them have been its inspiration. There is not space enough here to acknowledge all the readers of the first book who wrote to me, from all over the world, with suggestions and comments, and in any case they have each received a personal letter of thanks. I hope their efforts will be discernible to them in the text.

I do feel impelled to thank publicly certain individuals whose contributions have been indispensable. Throughout the compilation of this volume Joan Borland of Ibrox and Joe Dornan of Cranhill kept up a constant flow of suggested material and without their input its scope would have been far narrower and its content less colourful. The staffs of The People's Palace and The Mitchell Library have been instrumental in resolving some of my doubts and shoring up my assumptions with fact.

The following Glasgow-connected writers have also been generous with their time and knowledge: Moira Burgess, Cliff Hanley, Carl MacDougall, William McIlvanney, Jack McLean, Stephen Mulrine, David Neilson, and Hamish Whyte.

To each and all goes my thanks but most of all to my wife, Alice, who makes things possible.

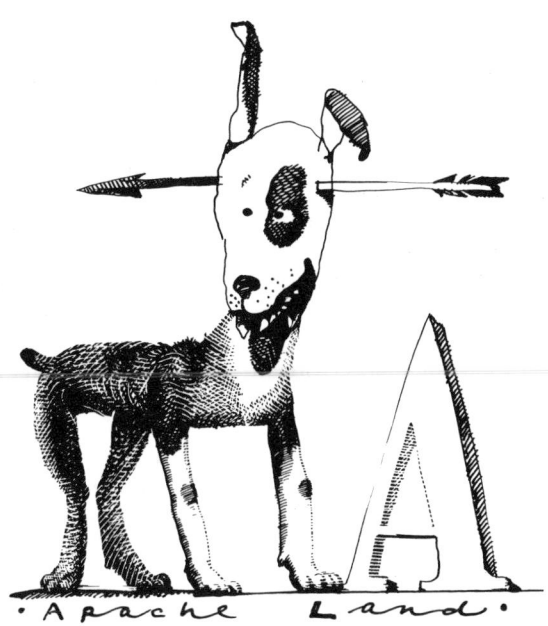
·Apache Land·

ah but An expression introducing an objection or contradiction: 'Time you were in yer bed.' 'Ah but Mammy said we could stay up fur Miami Vice.'

Ally Park A nickname for Alexandra Park, a public park in the city's East End: 'Ally Park's as near as you've ever been to the country.'

am Ah right am Ah wrang? A conversational interjection seeking the listener's agreement. The question is, of course, purely rhetorical as no-one actually expects to be told he is wrong: 'There's no way that shower are goany win the league — am Ah right am Ah wrang?' 'You're right, son.'

Annacker's midden A proverbial place of mess or disorder: 'Ah wid ask ye in, Mrs Eh, but they weans've goat the hoose lik Annacker's midden.'

Who was Annacker, and what was so special about his midden? Ask Glaswegians of a certain age and they will tell you that Annacker's was a baker's shop; or they might say it was a butcher; another will insist it was a sausage factory. As to where it stood, some will say at Bridgeton Cross; others remember it at Glasgow Cross; or no, definitely Woodlands Road.

The truth of it is that everyone is right. Annacker's was a firm of pork butchers, sausage makers, and ham curers. Founded in 1853, at its height it was a chain of sixteen branches all over the city. The company also owned a sausage factory, the last location of which was Napiershall Street (near St George's Cross). The People's Palace has in its collection the shop sign from the Bridgeton Cross branch.

The theory of how this worked its way into the dialect is as follows. Like any food retailer Annacker's had a certain amount of substandard or damaged stock unfit for sale that was thrown out as refuse. It is said that the hungry poor were given to raking through Annacker's bins for anything edible and the mess that this inevitably left gave rise to the phrase.

While Annacker's went out of business in 1942 the phrase the firm inspired lives on in everyday use as a perfect example of how language clings to an expression that is vivid and memorable long after its origin is forgotten.

Annie Rooney This name is used to refer to a fit of bad temper: 'If she finds out you broke that clock she'll have an Annie Rooney.'

I have been unable to discover if there was ever an actual person of this name but I allow myself to imagine a red-headed Irishwoman shouting the odds at somebody.

Apache land A wry description of any rough or undesirable area: 'That's real Apache land where he stays. The dugs go roon in packs fur self-protection.'

appetite Someone who is eating in a particularly hearty manner may have it said of him that **he's lost his appetite an found a horse's**.

arse **Kick your own arse** is Glasgow's more emphatic version of kick yourself: 'Imagine the big chooky tippin us the winner an no backin it hissel — he'll be kickin his own arse the night.'

On the other hand, or foot, an inept football player may be dismissed by the phrase **he couldny kick his ain arse**.

A rude way of telling someone to get lost or stop annoying you is to say **away an take a run up ma arse**, in the firm belief, I'm sure, that no-one will actually comply with the invitation.

If you find that another person's taste in clothes, decoration, music, etc. is not in harmony with your own you might express your disapproval by saying **your taste is in yer arse**.

Someone who is very nervous or on tenterhooks may have it said of him that his **arse is nippin buttons**.

arsed To say you **canny be arsed** means you can't be bothered, can't raise the energy or enthusiasm: 'He wants tae go tae the pictures the night but Ah canny be arsed.'

away A shortened form of away wi it, or away in the heid, meaning crazy or stupid: 'The guy's no right in the heid, pal, he's away.'

away a place A delicate euphemism for dead: 'Gauny slow doon, ya heidbanger! Ah thought Ah wis away a place there.'

aye When said in an ironic tone of voice this means that you don't in the least believe what you have just been told. It can be said on its own or with rhyming additions such as **aye, Hawkeye; aye, hooch-aye; aye, Popeye; aye, doogie-eye.**

A variation is **aye, that eye** which is accompanied by pointing a finger at your own eye. At its most economical nothing at all need be said if you put your forefinger to your lower eyelid. Perhaps all this is related to the old-fashioned expression 'all my eye' meaning nonsense.

This affirmative also turns up at the ends of queries that exemplify what I call the Self-answered Question eg 'Is that your pint, aye?' or 'You comin wae us tae Balloch, aye?' The opposite of this is seen in such constructions as 'You'll no be wantin any dinner, naw?'

B.1 or Bee Wan To do a **Bee Wan** means to go to another place, head off in another direction: 'When Ah seen the big moocher shufflin alang Vicky Road Ah done a Bee Wan up Torrisdale Street.'

This expression derives from a piece of civil service paperwork. When a person first registers as unemployed it is the usual practice that he receives no money for the first week from the Department of Employment. He will be issued with form B.1 and told to take this to the DHSS and apply for Supplementary Benefit.

You couldn't find a better example of the influence on the dialect of the sad and inevitable subculture fostered by mass unemployment.

babes To say that something is **the babes** means that it is excellent, just what's required: 'That soup's the babes, Mammy!' An even more affectionate or appreciative version of this is **the wee babies.**

I would say that this may well be a product of rhyming slang, with babes being shortened from babes in the wood, ie good.

back The phrase **all over the back** is used when referring to something that is typical of a particular person: 'Wouldny gie ye the len ae a quid fur yer bus? Aye, that's him aw ower the back.' Also used by a person detecting a physical resemblance between two relatives: 'You're your auld boy aw ower the back.'

backie-in *or* **backsie-in** In an informal football game where one side has a player more than the other the outnumbered team may be allowed by agreement to have a **backie-in**, ie a player who can double as both goalkeeper and ordinary player: 'OK, yous get Maradona here an wee Boabie'll go backie-in fur us.'

backside furrit Backside forward, from back to front; like inside out this means thoroughly or intimately: 'Never mind whit he says. Ah'm tellin ye Ah know this joab backside furrit.'

bad mastard A deliberate spoonerism coined to (narrowly) avoid using foul language: 'Watch where ye're gaun wi that, ya . . . bad mastard, ye.'

baddie To **take a baddie** means to take a bad turn, feel suddenly unwell: 'Is that right your aul fella took a baddie comin oot the subway?'

badness To do something **for badness** means to do it from mere spite, to be awkward, or for mischief's sake: 'The wee horror flung hissel aff that waw fur badness just cause Ah widny pay attention tae um.'

bag To **bag** someone is to give him the sack: 'That's yer last warnin, pal. Any merr a this an ye're bagged.'

-bag This is a common suffix always used to label a person who epitomises the undesirable qualities of the word it is attached to, such as *crap-bag*, coward or *grot-bag*, unpleasant or dirty person. I have even heard *stum-bag* (styoom-), an idiot, which is a development from *stumer*.

baggy Aggie An insulting name for any female wearing ill-fitting, over-large clothes: 'Hey, baggie Aggie, did ye get that dress at Black's of Greenock?'

bag up Any drink that is very fizzy and thus fills your stomach with gas is said to **bag you up**: 'That Canadian beer fair bags ye up.' 'Ah wis that bagged up wi ginger Ah couldny eat ma dinner.'

Balgray, the A familiar name for Balgrayhill, a district on the north side, near Springburn: 'Ah'd like tae go up an see ma wee niece in the Balgray but Ah'm no fit fur that hill.'

bare week A week's work without any overtime or earned bonus: 'Ah've tae pit in a Setterday an Sunday tae get near whit he pulls in fur his bare week.'

bastartin A piece of foul language whose inventiveness lies in making a noun appear like a verb: 'Ach, chuck the bastartin thing in the bin!'

baw-hair A pubic hair, regarded as the very narrowest of fine measures: 'Whit haunless bampot drapped that hammer? That wis a baw-hair aff stovin in ma skull!'

baws Balls, that is, testicles. These turn up in various common phrases, such as one rather rude way of telling someone he is talking nonsense or is incapable of doing something: 'Yer baws are mutton.'

bazooka'd A slang term for drunk: 'Whit a tube, eh? It's only gone nine an he's bazooka'd already.'

beans **Cool the beans** is an exclamation meaning calm down, take it easy, etc: 'Jist sit on yer backside an cool the beans tae Ah finish giein ye the story.'

Bella, the A nickname for Bellahouston Park, a large public park in the south west of Glasgow: 'This is a good yin of me an yer Mammy at the Bella yon time the Pope wis oan.'

belly Someone who is considered to speak without thinking or to talk a load of rubbish may have it said of him that **he just opens his mouth an lets his belly rumble.**

bender mender A slang term for a stiff drink used as a hair-of-the-dog hangover cure: 'Get this doon yer thrapple. Ye look lik ye could do wi a bender mender.'

berrs, the A term used to describe anything excellent: 'This lasagne's the berrs!' It may be that this is a shortened form of the similar expression *the berries.*

better Two local ways of saying that something is better than nothing are:
better than a slap in the face with a wet haddie.
better than a skelp in the baws wi a pun a wet tripe.

big This is used to mean older, senior, or most important, as in the **big school**, secondary school: 'Don't tell us ye're gaun tae the big school noo, hen?'; the **big team**, the first team: 'The boss says Ah'll soon be ready fur a run in the big team'; the **big picture**, the main feature in a cinema bill: 'Whit time's the big picture oan at?'

Big lassie is a child's term of address to an older girl or young woman: 'Hey, big lassie, you goat the right time?'

Big Aggie's Man A mythological character on whom anything you would rather not admit to can be blamed: 'I wisny me — it was Big Aggie's Man.'

The original Big Aggie and her man appeared in a popular song of the 1930s.

big an heavies A nickname for Benson and Hedges, a proprietary brand of cigarette: 'Ah'll take wan a yer big an heavies if ye're offerin.'

binnies A familiar term for binmen or refuse collectors: 'She always leaves out a few cans of beer for the binnies at Christmas.'

birlin A Scots word meaning spinning, often used locally to mean drunk: 'Sumdy'll need tae see Gus up the road. The man's birlin.' There are a couple of more elaborate forms of this, such as 'his eyes are birlin' or 'the eyes are birlin in his heid.'

bit[1] A local word for one's home, or home area: 'Emdy fancy nickin back tae ma bit?'

A **wee red bit** is a light for your cigarette from the glowing end of someone else's already lit one: 'Naw, Ah've no goat any matches, but Ah'll gie ye a wee red bit.'

bit[2] To **take the bit out of** someone means to exhaust him, leave him out of breath: 'These stairs of yours fair take the bit out of me.'

Black Street The proverbial name and location of a clinic that, amongst other things, is a treatment centre for veneral disease: 'Ah wis just tellin yer girlfriend here that Ah've no seen ye since Ah bumped inty ye at Black Street the other week.' A dreadful insult, whose implications will be obvious, is to call someone a **Black Street case**.

bladdered A slang term for drunk: 'Here, are you drunk?' 'Naw, missis, naw . . . Ah'm afraid Ah'm pure bladdered.'

blast A taste or portion of something, particularly of alcoholic drink: 'See's another blast a that malt, big yin.'

blitzed Yet another word meaning drunk: 'Let's get blitzed again, like we did last summer.'

blooter As well as to kick this word is widely used as a term of general excess. For example, if you quickly spend a sum of money you may be said to have 'blootered the whole lot'. A **blooter** is a quickly done, sloppy job: 'Look at the runs in this paintwork; this's been a blooter of a job.' A **mental blooter** is a spree of any kind of excessive behaviour, not solely applied to heavy drinking: 'He's giein it the mental blooter tae get the decoratin done fur her an the baby comin hame.'

blaw The Scots word for blow, used locally as a slang term for marijuana: 'Is he bevvied, or what?' 'Naw, too much a the blaw.'

blue job A slang term for a five-pound note: 'That wis a blue job Ah gave ye, by the way, no a wancer.'

boardies When children are playing on a rope swing, ie a knotted rope hung from a tree branch, a child who seeks permission to join others already hanging on shouts: 'Boardies?'

boat The phrase **just off the boat** implies that the person so described has not long arrived as an immigrant from Ireland and is therefore stereo-typed as naive and unsophisticated in the ways of the western metropolis. It is often applied to those who have a look of being of Irish descent: 'Is that her aul fella? He looks like he's just off the boat.'

boilermaker A disparaging name for a medical practitioner regarded as being insufficiently gentle in his handling of patients' bodies: 'That's never a doactor, that. He's a boilermaker.'

bold To put the words **the bold** before someone's name can be a way of say-ing that you think he is cheeky or pushy, although this is often used ironi-cally to mean exactly the opposite: 'Well, if it isny the bold Arthur! Is it no past your bedtime, son?'

bonnie A local word for a bonfire: 'Mister, kin we go through your skip fur stuff fur wur bonnie?'

boona To **give it the full boona** means to go the whole hog, hold nothing back, particularly in a situation in which you may as well be hung for a sheep as a lamb: 'Are ye for the off after this pint or are we gauny gie it the full boona the night?'

This term entered the dialect from Indian and Pakistani restaurants where if you order a dish called a boona (as in lamb boona, etc.) you will be served your meat in a thicker, drier sauce than in a plain curry. In some restaurants it is possible to order a half boona or a full boona, depending on how the size of your eyes is related to the size of your belly.

boot To **boot** someone is to sack him: 'Whit're you daein back here? Did Ah no tell ye ye're booted?'

boss In some schools, a nickname for the headmaster: 'Sky it! Here the boss!'

bought A **bought house** is the local term for one that is privately owned rather than rented: 'Aye, movin doon south wis the best thing they ever done — they stay in a bought hoose noo, ye know.'

bowfies A local term for head lice: 'Miss, Ah'm no sittin next tae him. His heid's full a bowfies, so it is.'

I'm sure there must be a connection between this word and *bowfin*, meaning smelly or disgusting.

brains One contemptuous way of referring to a no-scoring draw in a football match is to say **nae brains each.**

brammed-up Dressed up in your best gear, done up to the nines: 'Whit a dump ae a place he picks tae bring us tae. It's a pure waste a time gettin brammed-up tae sit in here.' This is obviously related to *brammer*, meaning anything excellent.

brassneck To **brassneck** it is to try to get away with something by a show of sheer confidence and nerve: 'If they ask ye for yer ticket jist brassneck it an say ye're with the band.'

breidsnapper A slang term for a child, emphasising the aspect of a constant necessity to keep it fed: 'That's her wi anither breidsnapper on the way.' This is sometimes shortened to **snapper.**

brekwist A local variant of breakfast. How the 'f' became a 'w' is anybody's guess: 'Ah like a bit a bacon fur ma brekwist oan ma hoalidays.'

brick A slang word for a pound sterling: 'Goany stake us a brick tae the morra?'

Brox, the A nickname for the Ibrox area in the south side: 'Youse gaun tae the Brox an aw? Moan we'll go haufers oan a Joe Baxi.'

Bubbly Babies Literally meaning crybabies, this is a disrespectful name for the Boys' Brigade. Another such cheeky interpretation of the initials B.B. is the **Bad Boys**.

bucket **To bucket** something is to throw it out, toss it in the bin: 'Ah knocked ma pan in gettin that report ready an aw he kin say is "Bucket that."'

Buckie A familiar name for Buchanan Street. A walking route through the city centre that has become a catch-phrase is 'Up Suckie (Sauchiehall Street), doon Buckie, an alang Argyle.' People often say this is where they are heading if in fact they have no particular destination in mind.

buly A slang term for an ambulance: 'Ye better pull in tae the side an let this buly by.'

bump[1] Another word for the sack, dismissal from your employment: 'Ah see wee Dougie goat the bump fae his work the other week.'

bump[2] A slang word meaning to swindle, fiddle, defraud: 'He lost his job as a Pools collector for bumpin the money.'

bundy A workmen's shelter, as on a building site: 'Ah know for a fact you've no stuck yer neb oot that bundy aw mornin.'

bunjies Another word for sandshoes: 'He's jumped in a puddle an soaked his bunjies, hell mend um.'

bunnet As we all know, this means a man's cap, but you may not know that to **do your bunnet** means to go off your head with anger: 'He'll do his bunnet if he disny find that ticket.'

bunnet-hustler A disparaging term for someone who plays up his humble working-class origins, especially one who does this from the comfortable position of being currently well-off or successful: 'Ah wish tae Goad that wee bunnet-hustler wid gie it a rest. He's no the only wan tae come oot a single end.'

burny Very hot to the touch or taste: 'Mind that iron, son, burny burny!' 'Can Ah get anither wan a yer sweeties, wan a the burny wans?'

burst This is often said in relation to a bank-note, meaning to use it to pay for something: 'Ye canny burst a twinty note just fur a paper.' 'Ah feel lik lashin oot. Aye, Ah could burst a fiver!'

A commonly heard threat of physical violence is 'Ah'll burst yer arse!'

To **burst your coupon** means to make your pools coupon lose by failing to supply the desired result: 'That's me finished wi St Mirren. That's two weeks in a row they've burst ma coupon.'

bus The cry **haud the bus!** means wait a minute, slow down, don't be hasty: 'Here, haud the bus. Yer shirt tail's hingin oot.'

Someone who is declining to accept repayment of a sum of money lent because he considers it not worth bothering about may say **Ah've lost merr runnin for a bus.**

buttie *or* **buttie-up** A walk in the company of an acquaintance: 'Wait a wee minute an Ah'll gie ye a buttie up the road.'

butts, the An old-fashioned term, still heard occasionally, for the Fire Brigade: 'Away you an get the butts, son, yer granda's set fire tae the kitchen.'

This derives from the water butts or barrels formerly carried to the scene of a fire.

That's you clamped!

Cally *or* **Carly** Nicknames for Carlsberg Special, a proprietary brand of strong lager: 'That's three heavies, two Callies, an a vodka an Irn Bru.'

cally dosh A slang term for money: 'Naw, Ah'm stayin in the night — a slight problem wi the cally dosh.'

campsie To **give it the campsie** means to do the housework in a quick cursory manner rather than painstakingly: 'OK then, I'll just give it the campsie and get you at the Light Bite at one.' If there is any connection between this expression and the Campsie Fells to the north of Glasgow I have been unable to discover it.

caramel To **drop a caramel** is a fairly whimsical slang phrase meaning to move one's bowels: 'Ah widny go in there fur a wee bit. Ah've jist drapped a caramel.'

Carndook A nickname for the Carnwadric area on the south side: 'Jump on a number forty-five tae Carndook an get the driver tae shout ye at Shawlands Cross.'

Carnegie The Scots-born self-made millionaire and philanthropist

Andrew Carnegie (1835 — 1919), whose name is still used to signify great wealth: 'A dishwasher ye're wantin noo? Who the hang d'ye think we ur, Carnegie?'

cattie Short for catalogue, particularly as used in mail-order shopping: 'Did ye get that coat oot the cattie?'

caunle A candle. The phrase **whatever lights yer caunle** is a local equivalent of 'whatever turns you on', as in: 'You sure ye want *his* phone number? Ach well, whatever lights yer caunle, hen.'

Central Glasgow Central Station: 'Ah'll get ye at Central at hauf seven, ootside R.S. McColl's.'

chib-mark A scar, as from a wound of a razor or knife: 'Check that for a hard ticket, eh? Chib-marks aw ower the coupon.'

choke To **choke down** something means to drink it despite having difficulty in swallowing, usually because you have already had enough to drink or because it tastes rotten: 'See him an that home-made wine a his? If ye manage tae choke doon wan gless he thinks ye're wantin anither wan.'
  On the other hand, to choke a bottle is to drink it quickly: 'The perr a them were chokin a bottle a whisky.'

chokin A description of someone suffering from an extreme thirst: 'Any danger of some service up this end of the bar? There's guys chokin up here.'

chuck The phrase **gie it a chuck** means to desist, stop what you are doing: 'If Ah've telt ye wance Ah've telt ye a hunnert times. Noo gie that a chuck, wull ye?'

clamp If you tell someone to **clamp it** you are saying be quiet, shut your mouth: 'You've got a big mouth for a wee boy, haven't ye, son? Well, clamp it!'
  If you deliver what you consider to be the final clinching word on some matter of dispute you might say to your adversary: 'That's you clamped.'

Clarence A nickname for someone who has crossed eyes: 'Wait till ye meet Clarence. Ye'll no know if he's lookin at you or two other fellas.'

This comes from a crosseyed lion of that name, star of a popular 1960s television series called *Daktari*.

Clint Eastwood A schoolkids' name for anyone who has a squint, obviously having an element of rhyming slang about it (Clint-squint): 'Miss, kin Ah sit nearer the blackboard? Ah'm Clint Eastwood.'

Clockwork Orange A nickname, perhaps more popular in the media than in the street, for the underground railway in its modernised incarnation, ie dating from its re-opening in 1979. Suggested, of course, by the orange livery of the trains: 'Ach, there's nae bus comin the day. Ah'm away fur the Clockwork Orange.'

closet To say to someone 'You're a closet' is a rather rude way of telling him he is talking rubbish; the suggestion being that you are like a toilet by virtue of being full of matter normally deposited therein.

Clyde Glasgow's river features in many catch-phrases. For example, someone who is considered unusually fortunate may have it said of him: 'He could fall inty the Clyde an come up wi a fish supper' or '. . . wi his pockets full a fish.'

In the well-known question 'do you think I came up the Clyde on a bike?' the bike can be replaced by various alternatives, including a water biscuit and a coolie boat.

If you are asked **what's that got tae dae wi Clyde navigation?** you may take this as a roundabout way of saying 'what's that got to do with the subject of discussion?' or 'I don't see the relevance of that remark.'

coaxie A variation of coal-carry, meaning a piggy-back: 'Ye'll need tae get doon, son. Ye're gettin a bit big fur a coaxie.'

coffin end A sharp corner of a tenement building: 'The hooses are always wee an poky in the coffin end.'

coo The Scots version of cow has various dialect uses. A **coo wi a gun** is an insulting way to describe someone considered clumsy or unskilful: 'Ye're lik a coo wi a gun wi that chisel. See's it ower here.'

A **coo's arse** can mean the end of a cigarette that has been over-moistened by saliva: 'OK, ye can have a drag a ma fag but don't gie it a coo's arse.' This can also mean any mess or botched job: 'Whoever hung this wallpaper made a coo's arse ae it.'

corn dobie A slang term for corned beef: 'Ah went an telt her Ah liked corn dobie fur ma piece an noo Ah get it every day.'

Corpy A nickname for Corporation, still used (even if technically incorrect) to describe local government: 'Ah wid get onty the Corpy aboot that hole in the pavement afore sumdy takes a purler.'

country pancake A city kids' term for a cow's dropping: 'Ah fell aff ma bike in Pollok Estate — right on tap ae a big country pancake!'

couped out A vivid description, presumably comparing the subject to something thrown on the ground, of someone unconscious or deeply asleep: 'The old guy couped out in front of the telly is ma faither.'

crash To **crash the lights** is to deliberately fail to stop at a traffic signal that has just turned to red: 'Aye, you crash the lights an we're aw meant tae sit here tae let ye by!'
  To **crash ahead** means to carry on with a task without delaying for any reason: 'You crash ahead wi the undercoatin till Ah get this door-frame sanded.'

crater-face An unkind name to call anyone whose face is pockmarked or scarred by acne: 'It's no make-up crater-face wants — it's Polyfilla.'

craw To **craw it** means to be afraid, chicken out: 'The wee brither's no comin. He's crawin it aff the Parkie.'
  A **crawbag** is a coward: 'Aye, that's right, run hame tae yer maw, ya wee crawbag.'

creep To **go at the creep** is to seek out female companionship: 'It's always the same when ye're out wi Doogie — wan or two jars then he goes at the creep.'

cremmy A slang term for crematorium. William McIlvanney gave me a story about a visit he made to a police mortuary. The attendant showed him the charred corpse of someone who had died in a fire and remarked: 'The relatives are wantin hauf-price at the cremmy.'

cuff A collective term for unattached and therefore presumably available women: 'No much ae a party that. There were nae cuff at aw.'
  Possibly this derives from rhyming slang for stuff, as in bit of stuff.

Curry Alley A nickname for Gibson Street, in the West End, famous for its large number of curry restaurants in what is a relatively short street: 'Ah need tae go doon Curry Alley haudin ma nose, cause if Ah get a whiff a the cookin Ah jist huv tae dive in fur a lamb boona.'

cut **Cut up** is a term used in driving that means to suddenly pull in in front of a vehicle you have just overtaken, often causing the other driver to brake: 'This diddy's flashin his lights cause he thinks Ah meant tae cut him up.'

Cut the nose off is another way of saying the same: 'Did ye see that big artic cut the nose aff us?'

Daniel gawpin oot the windae. / Must be love, eh? / Look at dreamy

dabbity A transfer, that is, a design printed on glossy paper that when licked and applied to the back of a child's hand will leave an image: 'Call that a tattoo? Ah've seen better dabbities.'

The word probably derives from the action of dabbing at the transfer on one's hand to make it print properly.

Dale, the A nickname for Leverndale psychiatric hospital: 'Did ye no know he's been in an oot the Dale fur years?'

Dallie, the A familiar name for the Dalmarnock area, in the East End: 'Ah comes aff the plane at Toronto, an ye know who wis the customs man? Wee Charlie fae the Dallie!'

damage A jocular term for a person's activity or doings, especially used in relation to someone enjoying himself in a boisterous manner: 'Naw, Ah'm no fur gaun hame yet — Ah've a lot merr damage tae dae the night.'

dancer[1] A slang term for a landing or floor in a tenement building, eg a **three-dancer** is the third floor; a **four-dancer** is the fourth floor: 'How is it whenever Ah've tae deliver a new machine it's always a four-dancer?'

A **tap-dancer** is, of course, not a variety turn in this context, but the top (tap) floor.

dancer[2] **Ya dancer!** is an exclamation of joy or enthusiastic approval: 'That's me got a treble up! Gaun yersel, ya dancer!'

dandruff **A mouthful of dandruff** is a highly pictorial slang expression meaning a head-butt in the face: 'You lookin fur a moothful a dandruff, sonny boy?'

dark o'clock This designates an unspecified late hour, but certainly after dark: 'Aw naw, it's dark o'clock an Ah'm meant tae be in early. The aul dear'll murder us.'

deck **To deck** someone is to knock him down with a blow: 'Rab jist stood up an decked the ignorant pig.'
   To **be decked** is to be laughing helplessly, in danger of falling on the deck: 'We were aw pure decked when we clocked ye wi yer suit oan.'

deefie 1. A cheeky name to call a deaf person: 'Hey deefie! Ah telt you tae get oot ma road.'
   2. To **throw** or **sling someone a deefie** is to deliberately ignore him, pretend that you didn't hear what he said: 'Aye, ye slung us a deefie the other night but Ah seen who was wi ye.'

delft In this part of the world this word applies not exclusively to earthenware of the type originating in Holland but to any crockery at all, thus giving rise to possible misunderstandings: 'Ye'll get aw the delft ye could want at The Barras, dead cheap an aw.'
   A stereotypical rag-and-bone man's cry is 'Delft for rags!'

denso A slang term for a stupid (dense) person: 'How'd a denso like that ever get his Higher?'

depth charge A powerful alcoholic drink, in particular a strong lager: 'You're gauny huvtae lay aff they depth charges if this is the state ye get inty.'

diddywasher A slang term, mainly used among schoolchildren, for a fool or useless person: 'That's another sitter that big diddywasher's missed!'
   I imagine this comes from being regarded as good for no more exacting task than washing a baby's dummy after it has fallen on the ground.

dillion (pronounced *dullyin*) A child's term for a single hard blow, espe-

cially one inflicted with the head: 'Big McConnell gied um a dillion.'
The word is also in wider use to mean anything exceptionally good: 'That new skateboard he goat's a pure dillion.'

ding a dent or bash: 'Ah see sumdy's pit a ding in yer bumper.'

dingy *or* **dinny** A schoolkids' word for the dining hall: 'Ah'll get ye at the dinny at the end a this period, right?'

div A slang word for a share in something, obviously shortened from division or dividend. **Square divs** means equal shares, fifty-fifty: 'Square divs if either of us wins this raffle, OK?'
Fair divs means fair shares, a just division, or more widely, that anything is considered reasonable: 'Aw c'moan, fair divs, Ah made the dinner, noo you dae the dishes.' 'Ah'll come back at hauf three an gie ye a spell, right?' 'OK, fair divs.'

Dizzy Corner A nickname for Boots' Corner, where many couples arrange to meet for a date and those unlucky enough to be stood up may be observed getting a dizzy.

dokey To **give it dokey** means to put one's all into something, give it laldy: 'The championship's wide open an the boays're goany gie it dokey noo that's the Cup oot the way.'
To **give someone dokey** is to give him a very hard time: 'Her maw gied her dokey fur gettin the wean's ears pierced.'

done The threatening phrase **you're done** means you've had it, you are doomed: 'See when Ah get a haud a you, pal, you're done.'

doof To **doof** someone is to hit him with the fist: 'He never says a word, jist reached ower an doofed the cheeky ratbag wan.'
A **doof** is a punch: 'You're askin fur a doof in the coupon an ye're gauny get it.'

doosh A slang word for the face: 'Ah wannered um right in the doosh.'

doowally A slang term meaning an idiot, someone not right in the head: 'There's me staunin oot in the rain lik a doowally an the door's open aw the time.'
This is probably related to the general British slang word *doolally,* which means crazy, off one's rocker.

double draw The surreptitious taking of two puffs on someone's cigarette when only one was agreed to: 'Gie's a wee drag, eh?' 'OK, but nae double draws, right?'

double dunter 1. Any event or undertaking consisting of two parts: 'Saturday night was a double dunter — the pictures, then a curry.'
2. Also known as **double dunt**, a double payment of benefit by the DHHS, usually because the next day the recipient is due to sign on is a public holiday and the office will be closed: 'Wait till ye see: the tube'll blow this double dunter in a week an then he'll be after me for a tap.'

double wide A slang description applied to someone who is extremely fly or not scrupulously honest: 'That boay a theirs is double wide — inty everythin, knows evrubdy.'

doughball A slang word for a fool: 'Haw, doughball! That's the wrang queue ye're in.'

dreamy Daniel A name applied to a distracted or absent-minded person: 'Look at dreamy Daniel gawpin oot that windy. Must be love, eh?'

dreep The Scots word for drip, often used in local dialect to mean someone who is tall and skinny or an insipid person: 'Ye want tae see the big glaikit-lookin dreep she's hingin aboot wi noo.'

Dublin To **kick up Dublin** means to create a fuss, complain vociferously. Yet another sideswipe at the proverbial hot temper of the Irish: 'Ma mammy's kickin up Dublin cause he disny want the wean christened.'

dumpie A soft or light blow, not seriously intended to injure: 'Whit's he greetin fur? That wis only a wee dumpie Ah gied um.'

dundy money A slang term for redundancy money: 'Ah say we should fight fur wur joabs. Yeez'll no be lang in runnin through yer dundy money.'

They always make me the edgyman cause Ah'm wee and fast...

eachy peachy A slang expression meaning a fair division, equal shares: 'Two tae me, two tae you, that's eachy peachy, intit?'

easy Usually pronounced *eas-ay*, this is an interjection used to greet any happy event or piece of welcome news: 'Late licence, is it? Easy! Here we go, boys!'

    The origin of this usage is in football, where the supporters of a team that is winning effortlessly will often exult in their dominance by chanting 'Easy! Easy! Easy!'

edgy A term used mainly by schoolchildren, meaning a lookout. To **keep edgy** means to keep a lookout: 'The wee man'll keep edgy till you an me have a fag.'

    An **edgyman** is someone appointed to keep a lookout: 'They always make me the edgyman cause Ah'm wee an fast.' If the edgyman spots some figure of authority approaching he gives warning by simply shouting 'edgy!'

    I assume the term derives from the nervously watchful condition of the lookout, who must feel 'on edge'.

eggs The phrase **all her eggs have two yolks** is said of anyone who is always bragging or can't abide to hear something praised without going one better: 'Know whit she says tae me? She says "Aye, yer new watch is very nice but ye want tae see the wan ma Robert brought me fae Gibraltar."' 'Never heed her — aw her eggs have two yolks.'

Eggy Toll A familiar name for Eglinton Toll, a busy road junction and landmark in the South Side: 'Ah says tae the driver "Wan an a hauf tae Eggy Toll" an he looks at us as if Ah'm a Martian or somethin.'

Elky A nickname for any male with the Christian name Alec. The phrase **get off your elky** means to get up and go, depart: 'Him? Ach he goat off his elky tae Aberdeen ages ago.'
The full form of this expression is **get off your Elky Clark** the last part of which is rhyming slang for mark, as in get off one's mark. The age of this usage is shown by the details of the man referred to. Alexander (Elky) Clark (1898-1956) was a famous Glasgow boxer, one in a long line of wee tough fighters.

Embos A nickname for Embassy, a proprietary brand of cigarette: 'Get us a packet of Embos an a Milky Bar.'

Embra A broad Glaswegian version of Edinburgh: 'Course Ah've been tae Embra — wance.'

emdy's game If you come across an informal game of football and would like to join in, the popular etiquette is to ask 'Is it emdy's game?' ie is it anybody's game, can anybody play?

ender When girls are playing at communal skipping each of the two who caw (swing) the rope is called an **ender**: 'You an oor Marie kin go enders tae start wi.'
A girl who gives up her turn at skipping because she prefers to caw the rope is called an **ever-ender**.

eppy Short for epileptic fit, as in to **take an eppy**: 'A boay took an eppy in the Music class the day.' The phrase is also used figuratively to mean a show of bad temper or rage: 'Big Bawjaws'll take an eppy when he sees what wee Tony wrote on the playground.'

eyes Bloodshot eyes are described pictorially as **eyes sewed wi rid threid**: 'Every mornin he comes in wi eyes sewed wi rid threid.'
Another phrase on the subject of tiredness is **my eyes are gaun thegither**, that is, I'm so tired that my eyes are crossing.

A face like a Halloween cake...

face Glaswegians must be terribly keen on personal beauty in their fellow citizens if the number of ways they have of describing an unattractive face is anything to go by. Here are some of the examples I have collected, and I'm sure the list is nowhere near complete:

a face like a burst tomato
a face like a chewed caramel
a face like a Halloween cake
a face like a melted welly
a face like a welder's binch (bench)
a face like a well-skelped arse

Other ways you might use to say that you find someone unpleasant to look at are:

ye could roughcast waws wi that face
ye could chop wood wi that face

Someone who suffers from acne or has a good crop of spots may be said to have **a face like a dartboard.**

A depressed-looking person may be told that he has **a face like a wet Monday.** If you have an air of pitifulness or look in need of tender loving care you may be described as having **a face that would get a piece at any windy.**

To **get a sore face** is to be beaten up: 'You better take yersel aff before ye get a sore face, wee boy.'

fair To **go like a fair** means to be very busy, bustling with activity: 'Ah've no had a sit-doon the day. The shoap's gaun lik a ferr.'

falsers An informal word for false teeth: 'No thanks, hen, Ah canny go the toaffees wi these new falsers.'

Fat Nan the Boxer A proverbial big eater: 'Nae wonder she's pittin on the beef — She's eatin like Fat Nan the Boxer!'
I have been unable to find out but I would love to know if this is based on a real person. Imagine: not only a female pugilist but a fat one at that. She must've been a big stoater.

fawnty A joke term for a car that is in a poor state of repair: 'He drives a Fawnty . . . fawin tae bits!'

Fire Brigutts A slang term for the Fire Brigade, probably an amalgamation of *brigade* and the older word *butts*: 'Oh aye, Ah wonder where the Fire Brigutts are headin tae up that road.'

fizz **A face like fizz** is an angry face, the face of someone who is not bothering to disguise his displeasure: 'She just sat there with a face like fizz and never said a word to anybody.'

flakie **to take** or **throw a flakie** means to lose your temper in a spectacular manner: 'The gaffer's gauny take a flakie when he sees this isny finished yet.'

flickie A slang word, short for flick-knife: 'Keep yer eye on the skinny wan. He carries a flickie in his jaiket poacket.'

floaters A collective word for small samples of what you have been eating that find their way into a bottle that you take a mouthful from: 'OK, ye can get a slug but don't gie us any a yer floaters.'

flute baun A band of flute or whistle players, as seen in Orange Walks and similar parades: 'Ah never peyed fur they music lessons jist so's you could jine a flute baun.'

folly *or* **foley** Local variants of follow: 'You jump in the aul boy's motor an foley us tae the airport.'

France A suggested destination for someone you would like to get rid of while not wishing to demean yourself by actually swearing: 'Ach, just you get tae . . . France, oot ma road.'

frontyways On the model of sideyways, this means front end first: 'Try it sideyways, an if it isny gauny go, take it frontyways.'

frozen snotter A horribly graphic term describing someone who has been out too long in cold, wet weather: 'She came tae the door like a wee frozen snotter . . . left her brolly at her work.'

Fustie A nickname for Furstenberg, a proprietary brand of imported lager: 'Ah'll get these. Fusties all round, is it?'

Never thought Ah'd see aul Charlie at the garden party. Must be in the grubber right enough...

gantin A slang word for stinking: 'How long is it since you had a wash? Ye're pure gantin.'

garbo Nothing to do with she who wanted to be alone, this is a slang term shortened from garbage and applied to anything considered contemptible: 'Ah'll no be back here in a hurry. Ah've never et such garbo in ma puff.'

garden party An ironic term for a drinking session on waste ground or in a park, as attended by down-and-outs, alcoholics, or simply those who have enough cash for some cheap strong wine or a couple of extra-strength lagers and have no place to drink in: 'Never thought Ah'd see aul Charlie at the garden party. Must be in the grubber right enough.'

Gaspipe, the A familiar name for Garscube Road, running between Cowcaddens and Maryhill: 'Whit buses go up the Gaspipe noo, sonny?'

GBH of the ear As I'm sure most people know, GBH is widespread criminal slang for physical violence, being short for grievous bodily harm. The local twist to this involves imagining damage done to the eardrums through being subjected to a long or loud harangue: 'Ye ask um how he's dain an ye get GBH of the ear. Wance he gets startit he willny shut up.'

gear The phrase **a bit of gear** refers to a sexually attractive woman: 'Ah widny mind gettin a grip a his big sister . . . a fine bit a gear.'

ginger The phrase to **bother your ginger** means to make an effort, show some concern or interest, but this is usually found in the negative: 'See that promotion he got? That could've been you but you wouldn't bother your ginger.'

On meeting a red-headed girl a patter-merchant might say: 'Hello Ginger, are ye still fizzin?' This is, of course, a double play on words, using ginger in the sense of any fizzy soft drink and as the nickname.

gink A slang word meaning smell: 'These denims a mine are ginkin.' 'There's some gink in that changin room.'

girth A fat belly, usually of the type produced by devotion to beer: 'Your aul boy's got some girth on him since he retired.'

glass cheque A jocular piece of slang for a bottle of any kind that has a deposit on it and is thus usable in lieu of cash when returned to a vendor: 'Gie's that glass cheque till Ah run out tae the ice-cream man.'

Glesga grin A slang term for a slash on the face: 'Let's see whit the Cockney wide boy looks like wi a Glesga grin.'

Glesga nod A slang term for a headbutt: 'Never mind arguin wi the diddy — gie um the Glesga nod.' This is also known as the **Glesga kiss.**

globe A local term for a light bulb: 'That's no anither globe went, is it?'

go-bi-the-waw Literally, go-by-the-wall, this is a disparaging name applied to a slow-moving or lackadaisical person: 'We'll miss that train if we've tae hing aboot waitin oan big go-bi-the-waw.'

Goldfinger A schoolchildren's nickname for any teacher whose excessive smoking is betrayed by heavy nicotine stains on his fingers: 'When I found out they called me Goldfinger I assumed it was something to do with my powerful dominating personality.'

gommy[1] To **run the gommy** is a local kids' version of running the gauntlet. In this case a boy is made to run between two lines of other boys who try to kick him as he passes: 'Pass it on: ootside the shed at playtime, that wee grass Muldoon's tae run the gommy.'

I think this comes from a mixture of an attempted shortening of gauntlet with overtones of *gommy*, meaning an idiot.

gommy[2] A local version of gammy, ie artificial, false, as in **a gommy leg**; or counterfeit, fake, as in **gommy money**.

Gourock This town on the Firth of Clyde features in a couple of proverbial phrases. **Away to one side like Gourock** means lop-sided, unbalanced, skew-whiff: 'Come here till I fix your hat; it's away to one side like Gourock.' This seemingly derives from the fact that Gourock is built mainly on one side of a hill.

Gourock and Greenock eyes means crossed or squinting eyes; the idea behind it being that one eye's looking at Gourock and the other at Greenock.

Govan This world-famous district of south-west Glasgow has long since made its mark on the dialect.

Good God in Govan is an exclamation or mild oath, invented no doubt for the sake of the alliteration rather than the likelihood of the burgh's being chosen as location for the Second Coming.

Sunny Govan is a nickname for the place, used mainly by its inhabitants, that typefies the Glasgow blend of love of your own patch tempered with ironic appreciation of its shortcomings.

What's that got to do with the price of Spam in Govan? is another of these elaborate smart ways of asking 'what's that got to do with the subject, how is this relevant?': 'He keeps layin it aff tae us aboot they Palestinians. Ah mean, whit's that goat tae dae wi the price a Spam in Govan?'

A or **the Govan kiss** is a slang term for a headbutt: 'He says he walked inty a door but Ah seen um gettin the Govan kiss ootside the chippie.'

Govanite The term for a native of Govan: 'Ma uncle Joe's the secretary of the Sydney Govanites' Association.'

granny To say **your granny!** in response to someone's statement is to imply that he is talking nonsense. In its fuller form the expression is used to precisely ridicule the other person's claim, as in: 'Ma big brother's a brain surgeon.' 'Aye, yer granny's a brain surgeon.' The most common catch-phrases along these lines are: 'Aye, an yer granny wis a cowboy;' and 'Yer granny on a scooter.'

grave-nudger A slang term for someone perhaps a little too long in the tooth: 'You should stick tae the over-30s nights alang wi aw the other grave-nudgers.'

greaser A slang word for that revolting thing a lump of spittle and mucus hawked up from the back of the throat and spat out: 'Some clatty article's gobbed a big greaser oan this windy.'

Green Lady A familiar name for a Health Visitor, originally from the colour of their uniform. Although nowadays they no longer wear a uniform this is still the general term in common use: 'She's friendly wi Mrs Sloan, ye know, her that's daughter's a Green Lady.'

grip The phrase **to get your grip** means to have sexual intercourse: 'He filled her up wi drink aw night so he'd be sure tae get his grip, an here it wis him that flaked oot.'

To **get a grip** of someone is to lay hands on him or her, with a view to embracing, cuddling, and if fortunate even further liberties: 'Check him in the Crombie. Ah widny mind gettin a grip a him.'

If you want to advise someone to calm down or keep the head, one rather disparaging way of putting it is to say: 'Get a grip of your liberty bodice.'

grot *or* **grotbag** A slang term for an unpleasant or dirty person: 'Get yer paws aff us, ya mockit wee grotbag!'

This is derived from the widely used British slang word *grotty*, meaning horrible, dirty, unattractive, etc.

growlers A slang word for sausages: 'You shove on some growlers an I'll butter these rolls.'

gubbing A thrashing or heavy defeat: 'The Jags took a gubbin aff Dundee United.'

gums To **bump your gums** is to speak, especially nonsensically, usually used when rudely asking someone to refrain from doing it: 'If you wid stoap bumpin yer gums fur wan minute Ah'd tell ye whit we're gauny dae.'

The insulting part is of course the suggestion that you are toothless and presumably senile.

gun To **gun** something is to use it up quickly, or, particularly in the case of drink, to swallow it rapidly: 'See that retsina? The only way to drink it is to gun it right back.'

. Away an run up ma humph .

hair ile Hair oil, a predecessor of today's hair gel, used in the dialect as a euphemism for hell: 'Whit the hair ile are ye rantin on aboot?'

hairy fit To **take a hairy fit** (sometimes shortened to **take a hairy**) means to go crazy with anger: 'The aul dear'll take a hairy fit if Ah'm late in again the night.'

hameldaeme Literally, home will do me, this mythical place name is used as a stock smart reply to the question 'Where are you going for your holidays this year?' It is particularly popular with people who can't afford to go anywhere.

hammer To **put the hammer on** someone is to ask him for a loan of money: 'Ah'm gettin scunnered wi him pittin the hammer oan us every Saturday night.'

To say **the hammer's on** means that there is trouble on the way, or that strict measures are to be enforced: 'The hammer's on just now, so keep your head down for a bit.'

A fine figure of a woman may be described as being **well hammered thegither.**

Hampden The name of Scotland's national stadium is used as a term for the final deciding game in a dominoes tournament: 'That's you against Aul Bert in the Hampden.'

hang To **hang someone's jaw off his face** is to slash him severely; 'If Ah get you Ah'm gauny hang yer jaw aff yer face, ya wee crawbag.'

hard-hearted Hannah A jocular name applied to any woman who is relatively strict in her dealings, definitely not a soft touch: 'It's no use asking hard-hearted Hannah for the morning off just because your budgie died.'

Apparently this comes from a song about 'Hard-hearted Hannah, the vamp of Savannah.'

hard-up This of course is British slang for short of money, skint. It does have a distinct local application in that when a girl is due to be married her friends or workmates often dress her up in a ludicrous fashion and parade her around the street or workplace banging on tins or anything similarly noisy. When a passing male is sighted he is greeted with cries of 'hard-up' and coerced into parting with some money, a kiss from the bride-to-be providing his reward.

hauf-scooped A slang term meaning somewhat intoxicated, rather than completely helpless. Presumably the latter condition might be described as 'scooped' although I have never heard this used: 'On yer bike, you. Ye're no turnin up hauf-scooped tae take me oot.'

haunbaw *or* **handball** This means to lift or carry a heavy load by hand rather than mechanical means: 'Never mind waitin on a fork-lift. The three ae us'll haunbaw this.'

Like many Glasgow vocabulary items this probably came from football terminology, in which handball is the deliberate illegal use of the hands (by any player other than the goalkeeper) to play the bal:.

Hawkheid A familiar name for Hawkhead Hospital, a psychiatric establishment near Paisley: 'You carry on this way an its Hawkheid you'll finish up in, ma lad.'

Someone considered daft may be accused of having **a heid like Hawkheid.**

head *or* **heid** To **head** is to leave, depart: 'If ye're wantin a lift Ah'm headin in five minutes.'

When someone has been successful at anything and has attracted praise for it, if he begins to think over-highly of himself he might have it said of him that **his head's gone.**

To **stick** or **put the heid on** someone is to butt him with the head: 'Boab went an stuck the heid oan the bouncer.'

The phrase **inty his heid wi a teaspoon** is a mock incitement to violence: 'Did you hear what that cheeky beggar called you? Go on, inty his heid wi a teaspoon!' The comparison is to smashing in the top of a hard-boiled egg.

If you want to tell someone that he is daft or scatterbrained you might say **yer heid's fulla broken bottles** or **wee motors** or **magic snowballs;** or **your heid's up the lum.** A phrase much used when advising someone to calm down is **keep the heid an Ah'll buy ye a bunnet.**

One way of saying that you have a hangover is **Ah've got a heid lik a sterrheid,** the idea being that your head is pounding as if it was a common landing in a tenement close that suffers the tramp of many heavy feet.

heard it! A sarcastic response to any statement or claim that you find hard to believe, the inference being that this is like an old joke that you have heard before: 'That's the first time I've ever been sick through drink.' 'Aye, heard it!'

heart To say that someone has **a big heart** means that he is very kind or unselfish in taking a lot of work or trouble on himself: 'Is that right he runs a youth club at the weekend as well?' 'Aye, he's a big heart, that man.'

heidnipper A slang term for a person who nips your head, ie scolds you or keeps on at you about something: 'His aul doll wis such a heidnipper he shot the craw doon tae London just tae get away fae her.'

here This is often used as an interjection to catch someone's attention: 'Here! Whit are yous up tae?'

It is also found as a shortened version of here is, as in: 'Here a train comin noo.' 'Here wee Joey on the phone.'

hey-you A slang term for a coarsely-spoken or insolent person: 'Ah don't like that crowd she's in wi at school. That wan she brought hame the day wis a right hey-you.' This derives from the use of 'hey you' by such people as the opening remark in a conversation with a stranger.

hing aboot A typically unromantic Glasgow expression meaning to go out with, have as one's boyfriend or girlfriend: 'Who ye hingin aboot wi since ye elbowed that Paul?'

hing aff This means get off, let go of me: 'Never mind yer wee cuddle ya ignorant pig, just hing aff, wull ye?'

hingin A graphic term meaning unwell, listless, feeling and looking below par: 'Ah don't know whit's the matter wi that boay a mines. He's been hingin aw week.'

hing oot One way of saying that you are very tired is **ma eyes are hingin oot ma heid.**
A **hing-oot** is an insulting slang word for a woman of easy virtue: 'Aye, she's no bad lookin . . . fur a clatty wee hing-oot.'

hit To **have a hit for yourself** is to think a lot of yourself, have an inflated idea of your own value: 'That boss a yours has got a real hit for himsel, hasn't he?'
If someone is likely to forcibly reject something you might offer it may be said that he will **hit you with it**: 'Nae use giein her Gancia if she wants champagne. She'd hit ye with it.'

hole A coarse word for the mouth, usually encountered on being told to close it: 'You shut yer hole till Ah rattle yer cage.'

holiday giro This is a slang term meaning the same as *double dunt*, in the sense of a double payment of benefit from the DHSS because of a public holiday, eg at The Fair. The phrase is sometimes used to mean any unexpected bonus: 'Ma big brother had a turn on the dugs an he bunged us a five-spot.' 'Hullo! Holiday giro!'

Home Ekies Short for Home Economics, a school subject: 'Try wan a they sausage rolls. Wee Brian made them in Home Ekies the day.'

hook To punch, with one hard blow: 'Haud us back, or Ah'm gauny hook um, hard man or no.'

howlin A slang word used to describe something that smells offensive: 'His boots were howlin so Ah slung them out in the close.'

howpin Another word for smelly: 'Ah'll need tae clean oot that fridge. Somethin's howpin in there.'

Huggy Loch *or* **Huggy** A familiar name for Hogganfield Loch, in the East End: 'He tried tae kid them on he wis an experienced sailor, when aw he'd sailt wis an oary boat on Huggy.'

humph A hump in one's back, used in a phrase of rude dismissal: **away an run up ma humph.** Another less than polite context for this is **stick it up yer humph.**

humphy-tumphy A mother's pet name for a child: 'Who's Mammy's wee humphy-tumphy, then?'

hunky-dunky A local variant of hunky-dory, ie fine, OK, alright: 'How's it gaun, big man, everythin hunky-dunky?'

hunnerjaikets A slang title for a person whose clothes are too big and are hanging off him.

huv, hud Local variants of have and had: 'Yous've no hud tae pit up wi whit Ah huv.'

huvtae *or* **huvtae case** A slang term for a necessary wedding, in which the celebrants 'have to' get married: 'It wis a dead quiet weddin — well, what can ye expect fur a huvtae case?'

He grabs a big dod a Irish Steak, slaps it between two outsiders an says "That'll need tae dae us till Ah get somethin tae eat"

Idleonian A rather old-fashioned term for someone who is considered to be out of work through choice rather than force of circumstances; a hangover from a time when jobs were easier to come by. Nowadays this is extended to mean anyone who appears to be lazy or is not pulling his weight: 'Oh aye, here am Ah knockin ma pan in an yous Idleonians can sit an read yer papers.'

indescribables A nickname for pakora (a popular starter served at curry restaurants): 'Ah'll have a double portion of yer indescribables an gie's plenty sauce, eh Jim?'

inky A school term, used by both pupils and teachers, for a felt-tip pen: 'Away and ask Mr Mackay for a packet of inkies and come right back here with them . . . and don't run!'

intit no? Literally isn't it not?, this is a common double negative most often used by a speaker seeking confirmation of some negative statement: 'It's nae use tryin tae get sense oot a that yin, intit no?'

Irish Steak A jocular nickname for cheese: 'He grabs a big dod a the Irish Steak, slaps it between two outsiders an says "That'll need tae dae us till Ah get somethin tae eat."'

Aw naw, here's a jam sandwich at ma back

jaiket To **haud the jaikets** means to be in attendance at some event without taking part, be an onlooker: 'Don't ask me what's gaun on. Ah'm only haudin the jaikets here, pal.'

This comes from the ceremony of a playground fight in which the two combatants have their square go while a supposedly neutral third party holds their jackets and any other restrictive accoutrements.

The phrase of warning **your jaiket's on a shoogly nail** is an indication that your position is not as secure as you might think; if you don't watch your step you might be out of a job: 'Late again, eh? You better screw the nut, sonny boy, cause yer jaiket's on a shoogly nail.'

jake A slang term for methylated spirits (as drunk by alcholic down-and-outs) or red biddy, ie cheap strong red wine: 'His guts must be rotten wi aw that jake he pours doon his thrapple.'

Jaked up means drunk, and **jaked out** means unconcious through drunkenness. Both terms have overtones of contempt as they imply that the individuals so described are winos: 'It's a wee bit rough an ready, this boozer. Ye'll maybe see wan or two guys jaked oot at a table.'

jakey A slang word for a down-and-out, especially one who obviously drinks lots of *jake*: 'This aul jakey comes up an bites ma ear fur the price of a cup a tea.'

jam sandwich A jocular term for a police car, from the Strathclyde force's livery of white with a red stripe along the middle of each side: 'Aw naw, here a jam sandwich at ma back.'

jammy dodger A proprietary brand of biscuit, consisting of two round pieces with jam in between. In the dialect this term is borrowed to mean someone considered very lucky: 'Big Dave won a motor in a raffle, the jammy dodger!'

jarred up Another expression meaning drunk, ie having swallowed a few jars (pints): 'It's a waste a time gettin jarred up before the gemme. Ye miss hauf ae it trailin back an forth tae the bog.'

Jeelie-eater A nickname for any inhabitant of the Vale of Leven, deriving from the time when Irish navvies constructing the Forth and Clyde Canal mainly lived in this area and were said to have jeelie pieces every day.

jeggie A slang word for lemonade or any soft drink, chiefly in use among schoolchildren: 'Ah'll gie ye a slug a ma jeggie fur wan a yer Rolos.'
By the sound of it, this word may have developed from *ginger*, perhaps via that strange phenomenon of slang, egg language. This involves disguising what one says by inserting the syllable 'eg' after each consonant of a word. This would make ginger 'jeginjeger', but this is only speculation.

jersey The phrase **sell the jerseys** (sometimes **jumpers**) means to sell out, betray your cause. The origin of this is, of course, football. Any team, but particularly a national side, that plays disappointingly may be accused by disgruntled fans of having sold the jerseys. In everyday life the phrase can be heard in contexts where someone is responsible for representing others: 'I would just like to remind the chairman the he and the other delegates are meant to be goin in to negotiate, no sell the jerseys.'

jimmies *or* **gymmies** A schoolkids' term for gymshoes or plimsolls: 'Ach Maw, these jimmies are gettin too wee fur us.'

Jimmy Johnstone When waiting at a pedestrian crossing in Glasgow and the light indicates that you may cross, you might hear someone say: 'C'mon, here's Jimmy Johnstone.' After all, I suppose the small-statured former Celtic football star is the nearest thing in life to a wee green man.

Such was this man's fame that any red-haired Glaswegian, especially a small one, is still liable to receive Jimmy Johnstone as a nickname.

jinkies To say that something is **the wee jinkies** is to describe it as excellent: 'Aye, yer granny's trifle's the wee jinkies, intit son?'

joiner A pejorative name applied to someone who joins a company drinking in a pub, partakes of several rounds, and disappears before it is his turn to buy: 'Aye, aye, here Wullie the Joiner comin in. Tell um it's his shout an see whit he does.'

jooks A slang term for trousers: 'Aw, c'moan, tell that stupit dug a yours no tae jump up oan the good jooks, eh?'

Poor Hughie's gaun aboot like a hauf-shut knife since that saft wee wife o his done a bunk...

Kamikaze, the A piece of CB slang for the Kingston Bridge, one of the busiest stretches of motorway in Europe, we are told: 'This is Night Nurse burnin rubber over the Kamikaze, headin into the Big Apple.'

Anyone who crosses the Clyde by this route at a rush hour will know why this nickname is apt.

kegs A slang term for trousers: 'Ah'll really need tae loss some weight. These kegs are stranglin us.'

Kensitas coupon The name of a gift voucher issued with a proprietary brand of cigarettes is borrowed in slang to mean anything having only nominal value: 'So you've got a degree in Philosophy? That's a Kensitas coupon in the big wide world.'

kerby (pronounced curby) A children's ball game in which a ball is bounced on the edge of the kerb: 'Me an Nicola were playin kerby ootside the close an this big motor nearly flattened us.'

kettlebelly A disrespectful nickname for anyone with a fat stomach: 'Hey kettlebelly, when are ye due?'

Khyber Pass Another nickname for Gibson Street (see **Curry Alley**):

'The quickest way to Byres Road is through the Khyber Pass an up University Avenue.'

kiltie This of course is a common Scots term for a man wearing a kilt, which appears in the local phrase **kiltie kiltie cauld bum**, a jibe shouted by children at someone thus dressed.

kipper's knickers, the A local equivalent to the bee's knees, etc, ie something wonderful: 'That yin thinks she's the kipper's knickers since Big Joe got aff wi her.'

knife To describe someone as going about **like a half-shut knife** means that he looks depressed or introspective: 'Poor Hughie's gaun aboot lik a hauf-shut knife since that daft wee wife a his done a bunk.'

The expression obviously arises from the image of a sad person walking bent over, looking at the ground, compared to a pen-knife with its blade neither fully open nor properly closed into the handle.

K.P. An abbreviation and nickname for the Kinning Park area of the South Side: 'Jeanie, here a couple from the K.P. that knew your mother.'

The pair a them wis lummed up before they even got tae the reception.

Lambies A nickname for Lambert & Butler, a proprietary brand of cigarette: 'Ah telt ye Lambies, no Bensons, ya doughball!'

like that The phrase **I was** (she was, we were, etc) **like that** often crops up in a conversational narration without meaning anything in particular. At one time it must have been accompanied by a pantomime of the relevant facial expression or bodily stance but it is now most commonly used without any demonstration or further explanation of the particular state referred to and must be described as mere verbal padding: 'She says "You're no comin wae us" an Ah wis lik that, Ah says "How've Ah no tae get?" an she wis lik that, an she says. . . .'

limit by asking for **a limit** of someone's cigarette it is mutually understood that you will be allowed a few draws on it (some say three, some four) and no more: 'Gauny gie's a limit oan yer fag, neebur, Ah'm gaspin.'

live up with A common phrase meaning to live in sin, cohabit with someone to whom you are not married: 'Aye, that's him that left his wife an weans tae live up wi some floozy fae Partick.'

loaded A descriptive term meaning full of the cold, having a runny nose, sore head, etc: 'Aw ya poor soul, ye're loaded. Away hame tae yer bed wi a hot toddy.'

long The expression **as long** means an unspecified but long time: 'Her wean's photie wis in that photographer's shop windy fur as long.'

The phrase **a long road for a short cut** is used when what is intended to be a quicker route seems to be actually longer than the usual way: 'I know it's a long road for a short cut but you miss all the traffic lights this way.'

loosie A slang word for a cigarette sold individually in a shop, as bought by those who are short of funds or under age: 'This guy'll sell ye a loosie nae bother, on ye go.'

luckies A nicely apt word for things of value found in rubbish bins, as hunted by midgie-rakers: 'Ah went doon tae the bins an here's this aul dosser gaun through them for luckies.'

lucky middens A slang term for bins where substantial luckies are likely to be found. Also extended to describe an area where such middens are the norm: 'I hear you've moved to Newton Mearns; up in the lucky middens now, eh?'

lummed up A slang term for drunk: 'The pair a them wis lummed up before they even got tae the reception.'

Lum, of course, is a Scots word for chimney, but apart from seeing someone as reeking with the fumes of alcohol the connection between drunkeness and chimneys escapes me.

lumps To **kick lumps out of** someone is to give him a good hiding: 'It does give one a poor impression of a hostelry when you enter the lounge to find two of the clientele kicking lumps out of one another.'

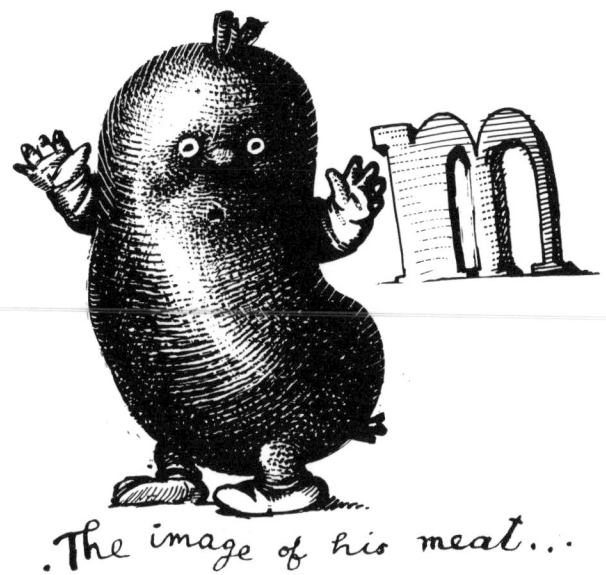

The image of his meat...

Maccy, the A nickname for Maxwell Park, a public park on the South Side: 'That's the pedal boats out on the Maccy pond. It must be Summer right enough.'

At one time it was said that you were not a fully-fledged Kinning Parker until you had fallen into Maxwell Park pond while hunting for baggies (minnows, that is, for those who don't know).

man The popular phrase **if he was a man at all** is used to mean if he had any common decency or the spark of human kindness: 'That big balloon could've given ye a run hame if he wis a man at aw.'

mate aboot This means to associate with someone as friends, have a particular person as your best pal: 'Aye, yer faither an me used tae mate aboot thegither when we were in John Brown's yard.'

meat It is often said of a child that is plump and healthy, well-fed looking, that he is **the image of his meat.**

mee-maws A nickname for the police, imitating the sound of a squad car's siren: 'Ah got wakened up in the middle a the night wi the mee-maws gaun doon the street.'

There's the old joke about the proud mother who has three strapping sons in the police force. Towards the end of their dinner she asks 'Who's fur merr puddin?' and hears in reply 'Me Maw, me Maw, me Maw!'

mental A **mental** is someone considered crazy or dangerously unpredictable: 'The driver stoapt the bus when this gang a mentals got oan at the Toll an widny pey their ferr.' To **throw a mental** is to lose your temper spectacularly.

mentions I am reliably informed that if a child is scrawling graffiti in the form of a list of names on a wall or any suitable surface, and one of his mates wants to be named in the roll of honour, he will be told 'Gie's mentions.'

This is sometimes shortened to **mensh**: 'How'd you no gie me an Hammy a mensh?'

mere A local form of come here, shortened in speech from the already compressed c'mere: 'Mere you! Whit's this you're sayin aboot me?'

message To **give someone the message** is to convince him of the error of his ways by means of physical force: 'Boy, you're goany get the message if Ah catch ye at this wee gemme again.'

mince A **pint of mince** is a slang term for a pint of Guinness, presumably from its relatively thick consistency: 'Ye canny take um anywhere. There we are sittin in the cocktail lounge an when the wee lassie comes tae take wur order he says "Gie's a pint a mince, dear."'

minder A small gift, often bought as a thank-you token for someone who has done you a kindness: 'She's been a right good neighbour over the years. I'll need to get her a wee minder before we go.'

minted A slang term used to describe anything you approve of or think is excellent: 'Ah hear ye passed yer test. That's minted, wee man.'

Perhaps this derives from the idea of a brand new shiny coin, newly minted, that stands out from the other dull coins in your change.

minute The phrase **this minute** means right away, right now: 'You get up they stairs this minute, ma girl.'

miss If you are angry with someone and are telling a third party exactly what you will do when you catch the offender, you might say **Ah'll no miss**

him or in its fuller form **Ah'll no miss him an hit the waw**: 'Ah'll be ready waitin when that boay comes in fae his work an Ah'm here tae tell ye Ah'll no miss um!'

Monday Book A common nickname for a book of DHSS benefit vouchers, especially one issued to single parents, so called because the vouchers are all dated payable on Mondays: 'The wean's been playing wi ma Monday Book an noo Ah'm gaun mental lookin fur it.'

monty A slang expression meaning hurry up or don't be silly: 'Where is the eejit? Hey you, monty!' This is a shortening of one or two similar phrases, the least offensive being **monty grips**, which literally means come on to grips.

moochie A schoolkids' word shouted as a warning when a teacher is approaching: 'Ah'm inty your heid if you shout moochie again when there naebdy comin.'
    Moochie-stiff is a more elaborate form of this, used as another name for the children's game of statues, in which at a given signal (ie a shout of 'moochie-stiff!') the players must freeze and stand perfectly still for a set time.

moony A slang word for a slow embracing dance, most commonly observed at the end of a disco when the romantic records are played: 'Ah'm that shy Ah hide in the lavvy when a moony comes oan.'

mooses' meat A nickname, fairly contemptuous, for cheese: 'Ah could never be a vegetarian. Ah need merr tae keep me gaun than mooses' meat an rabbit fodder.'

mortalled Another word for drunk, a local variant of the Scots term *mortal*: 'He tries tae tell us he only hud wan or two. Away, Ah says, mortalled wisny in it!'

Mount, the A familiar name for the Mount Florida area in the South Side: 'Ah liked it when we stayed up in the Mount . . . it wis a real wee community.'

mouth music A term among Glasgow Highlanders meaning deedling, or the singing of a tune using meaningless words to take the place of instrumental sounds: 'Gie Big Sandy anither hauf an he'll mibby gie us a blast a the mouth music.'

movin Moving, a descriptive adjective applied to someone or an area of someone's person that appears to be infested with lice: 'Ah'd tae sit next tae this poor wee soul at the doactor's. Nae jaiket nor nuthin, an his heid wis movin.'

Sampson was a strongman,
he lived on fish an chips.
He went along the Gallowgate
pickin up the nips

-nae *or* **-ny** Literally meaning not, this is a negative suffix common enough in Scots, as in *willny, cannae,* etc. It is used on its own by local children to contradict the last thing said to them, as if adding the negative ending to a word the speaker has used: 'Right, you're comin hame this minute, so ye are.' '-Nae!' 'You are so!' '-Nae!'

This kind of argument is not only maddening but invincible if persisted with, as there is nothing that you can say that can't be thus negated. You either give up or resort to stronger measures.

nae nae kiddin An emphatic insistence that you are telling the truth, used especially by children. It can also serve as a question, meaning you're not having me on, are you?: 'Look, Ah'll definitely get ye in fur nuthin.' 'Nae nae kiddin?' 'Nae nae kiddin.'

neb A cheeky person is often described as being a **wee neb**: 'That's enough oot a you, ya wee neb. Just keep yer face shut, right?'

neck To **get** or **take a red neck** means to be embarrassed to the point of blushing: 'Ah get a red neck every time that wean opens his mouth.'

Someone who sees this happen may make the observation **what a neck**! or describe the sufferer as being **necked**: 'Ye want tae have seen the beamer she got . . . she wis pure necked!'

need The phrase **ye wouldny need** . . . is often used at the beginning of statements that mean 'it is as well that you are not . . .', as in: 'Ye wouldny need tae be easy offended when ye hear the language ae um.'

neither Used in forming additional reinforcing statements at the end of a negative remark, as in: 'He'll no be away aw day, neither he will.'

newp When decimal money was introduced in the early 1970s everything was counted in new pence, which was typically and immediately shortened to **newps**. Although no longer in common everyday use you will still hear the word in certain fixed contexts, such as a twenty-pence piece being called **twenty newps**: 'Any a yous goat twinty newps fur this parkin meter?'

nip 1. **To nip** someone can mean to borrow money from him: 'Ah'll see if Ah can nip the brother fur a ten-spot.'

Someone who is trying to secure such a loan is described as being **at the nip**: 'Kid on ye don't see um. He'll be at the nip, sure as guns.'

A person who is always borrowing money may find that he is given a warning label to his name: 'Don't tell us ye lent a fiver tae Jimmy the Nip?'

2. **To nip** a cigarette is to put it out by pinching the lit end, usually with a view to smoking the remainder later on: 'Never mind yer fag, we've no got time. Nip it an stick it behind yer ear.'

A nip can be a partly-smoked cigarette that has been pinched out in this way or a simply a cigarette-end thrown away, as commemorated in the following delightful rhyme:

Samson was a strongman,
he lived on fish an chips.
He went along the Gallowgate
pickin up nips.

nip nipsies This is roughly equivalent to 'snap!', ie a catch-phrase said whenever someone sees a coincidence, such as two people having, doing, or saying the same thing: 'Nip nipsies! Ah've got a skirt the exact same as that.'

The explanation lies in the full formula which is **nip nipsies, nae nipsies back**. The speaker accompanies the words by physically nipping the other person and is, of course, made safe from retaliation. I would suggest that the rationale of this is to claim that whatever it is that is in common was your idea first and that any good luck obtainable from the coincidence can be appropriated by the first person to speak the ritual words.

nippie A brief or quick excursion: 'We'll do a wee nippie inty the bookie's on the way back.'

Nitsie, the A nickname for Nitshill, a housing scheme in the South Side: 'It's gauny be some night — the boys fae the Nitsie are aw comin.'

no honey A term used to stigmatise someone (male or female) who is considered lacking in physical beauty: 'That yin thinks he's God's gift, an he's no honey either.'

noise To noise someone up is to deliberately provoke or irritate him: 'Dae Ah get the impression you're noisin me up, shorty?' This originated as a motoring term meaning to sit behind another car at a traffic light and rev your engine in a supposedly intimidating manner.

Nollie, the A local nickname for the Forth and Clyde Canal, which passes through the north side of the city: 'Ah've telt them tae Ah'm sick no tae play doon the Nollie. There were a wee boay near droont the day.'
This comes from a shortening of a local pronunciation of canal, ie *ca-nawl.*

no real Literally, not real, this is used to mean indescribable, outrageous, insane, unbelievable, and so on: 'Did ye hear that wee bampot diggin up the Big Man? The boay's no real.'

nose Someone who has an excessively pointed or beak-like nose may attract a comment like: 'The last time Ah saw a nose like that it wis openin milk boatles.'

nuchin Pronounced with the ch as in 'loch' this is a local variant of nothing, popular perhaps because the ch sound lends it a vehemence lacked by the standard form.

nugget A slang word for a pound coin: 'Here, Ah'll get this. Ah've a poacket full a nuggets Ah'm tryin tae get rid ae.'

numb Another slang term meaning drunk: 'Ah could play this tune even if Ah wis numb; in fact, Ah have done.'

Numbies A nickname for Players' Number Six, a proprietary brand of cigarette: 'Is that you back on the Numbies, aye?'

numpty An idiot: 'How is it I get all the numpties in my class?'

numshie Another word for idiot: 'What Ah don't get is how the numshie goat a joab in here in the first place.'

nyuck A disparaging name for anyone you dislike, for whatever reason: 'That wis a right shower a nyucks sittin in fronty us at the ballet last night.'

. An oyster fur yer granda .

obs A local abbreviation of objections, most commonly heard in the question **any obs?** which can be fairly belligerent, in fact defying anyone to disagree: 'Right, it's ma motor, an Ah say we're gaun tae Largs. Any obs in the back seat?'

on To say to someone **you're not on** means there is no chance of that, I will not be complying with your wishes: 'If ye think Ah'm gauny carry the can fur this baws-up ye're not on, sunbeam.'

onion bag A football journalists' cliché for the net of a goal: 'The boys in blue rattled three into the onion bag.'

oot scoot A phrase of dismissal, usually said to children who are in someone's way: 'Here, let me into that cupboard, weans. Oot scoot, beat it!'
This probably comes from a children's game in which players are eliminated in turn by means of a chant ending 'oot scoot, you're oot'.

open In tenement houses when a child enters the close-mouth and wants to warn his parents that he is coming up the stairs he may shout the word 'open' or even spell it out 'O-P-E-N'. The idea is to have the door already open for him whether because it is too cold to hang about on the stairhead or because the close is dark and scary for a child.

oranges **Horse's oranges** is a term sometimes heard for horse droppings: 'If he spies horse's oranges lyin in the road he's out like a shot to snaffle them for his garden.'

ovies A familiar abbreviation for overalls: 'Aw maw, ye never washed ma ovies fur us!'

oxter This, of course, is a Scots word for armpit, and it appears in a local phrase of rude dismissal: 'Away an bone-comb yer oxters.' I take this to mean that you are implying that the person addressed is infested with body lice.

The aroma arising from sweaty armpits is sometimes referred to as **oxter-guff**, a term both succinct and vivid but unlikely to feature in a deodorant advert.

oyster A mouth-stretching delicacy obtainable from ice-cream sellers, consisting of two round shallow containers (like two halves of an oyster shell) made of the same stuff as wafers. One half is filled with ice-cream and the other placed on top to seal it. As this is far from being enough for the infamous Glasgow sweet tooth, one of the half-shells already contains a portion of artificial cream and is partly coated with coconut-sprinkled chocolate: 'Run out to the icey an get us aw a pokey-hat — an ye better get an oyster fur yer granda.'

A bum like a peemet...

Paisley The phrase **get off at Paisley** means to practise *coitus interruptus:* 'He said it wid be awright, he wid get aff at Paisley, an now look at us!' This idea of 'not going all the way' is based on a train journey to Glasgow back from the Clyde Coast, Paisley being the last stop before Glasgow Central.

Pally Ally A nickname for pale ale, being a deliberate mispronunciation of the words: 'If the Exports are me an Phil's, the lagers are Irene's, whose are the Pally Allies?'

pan **To pan** something is to break or burst it: 'Mind the time ye panned oor windy in? Aye, ye always took a good penalty kick.'

panhandler A slang word for someone who is always scrounging, attempting to borrow money or goods: 'Ah know he's a pure panhandler, but it's nae loss whit a freen gets, Ah always say.'

Pansy Potter A nickname bestowed on any female who performs a task requiring some physical strength: 'Look at Pansy Potter humphin they suitcases up the stair hersel.'
　　This comes from 'Pansy Potter, the Strongman's daughter', apparently a cartoon character in a children's comic.

pap A fool or soft character: 'Imagine a lassie a mines gaun aboot wi a pap like yon.'

Parly Road A familiar name for Parliamentary Road, in the city centre: 'Her man goat knocked doon wi a blue bus in Parly Road the other week.'

Partick The name of this district on the north-west side of the Clyde is found in the proverbial phrase **before the Lord left Partick**, meaning a very long time ago: 'Her faimly's steyed up this close since before the Lord left Partick. We're in this buildin twinty year an we're still the new folk tae her.'

Why Partick should be so singled out as God-forsaken I'm not at all sure, unless it's something to do with the area's high density of Glasgow University students.

pea If you go about wearing a hat that is too small for you, you may attract a remark like: 'That hat's like a pea on a dumpling.'

The same vegetable features in an unkind comparison used to describe an overweight person: 'His heid's like a pea on a mountain.'

A phrase of rude dismissal incorporating peas is **away an pap peas at yersel** or **away an pap peas at yer granny**, although why the old soul should be subjected to such a bombardment is beyond logic.

pelmet Someone whose backside is regarded as sticking out somewhat may be said to sport **a bum like a pelmet.**

picture An old term still in use for a cinema film, as in: 'That wis a rerr picture we saw on Setterday night, eh?'

piece If a child asks for a piece (ie a sandwich) and his mother has bread but nothing to put on it, he may be told he can have a **piece 'n' breid.**

pig A cruel term for an unattractive female: 'Hey Sammy, that wis a pure pig ye were winchin the other night.' An even more extreme form is **pig wi knickers.**

If males are on the hunt for talent and they assess the pub or disco they are in as being deficient in that respect they may decide the place is a **pigs' ballroom.**

pimps *or* **pimpsy** A slang word, most common among schoolchildren, describing anything considered easy to accomplish: 'Is that aw we've tae dae? That's pimps!'

This probably comes from a shortening of simple-pimple.

pint dish A slang term for a pint glass: 'Imagine drinkin Martini oot a pint dish. You've goat nae class, huv ye, ya toerag?'

pish A local version of piss. Someone who is seen as talking rubbish may be told: 'Ye talk a lot a pish.' **Pished**, of course, means drunk: 'Here, Ah'm pished. Stick ma car keys behind the bar an don't gie us them even if Ah threaten ye.'

pixie A slightly old-fashioned term for a young girl's woolly hat, usually tapering to a point: 'She's that nice in her wee Brownies uniform wi that wee pixie her granny knittit.'

plab A nicely onomatopoeic word for a cow's dropping: 'Ever stepped on a big coo's plab wi sandals on? It gets aw in between yer toes.'
The term can be used for other varieties of excrement, however: 'You're oot enjoying yersel an Ah'm stuck in here up tae the elbows in plabby nappies.'

play The phrase **Ah'm no playin** is often used by a petulant child withdrawing from a game because it has become too rough, the rules are not being respected, or any other reason: 'Is she tae get a game? Right, Ah'm no playin!'
This also turns up, slightly changed, when a child has fallen out with some of his friends. He will rebuff them by saying: 'Ah'm no playin wi yous.' As with many childhood expressions, these are often used by adults in jocular contexts.

pleckie A slang shortening of plectrum, ie a guitar pick: 'See's ower that pleckie till Ah batter oot wan we aw know.'

plum duff A slang expression meaning pregnant: 'It's murder polis in the hoose the noo. The wee sister's plum duff.'
This is obviously related to the similar slang term *up the duff*.

plunge To **plunge** someone is to stab him: 'Mind that rammy ootside the disco last night? Ah hear a boay goat plunged.'

polis office (pronounced *oafis*) A local term for a police station: 'Ah'm phonin the polis office if yous don't turn doon that racket.'

Polomint City A nickname, originally coined by CB enthusiasts but now in wider use, for East Kilbride, deriving from the large number of roundabouts encountered when driving through it: 'He wis last seen in Polomint City tryin tae get onty the Motherwell road.'

polute A deliberate distortion of the word polite, used mockingly in reference to anyone considered snobbish or excessively formal: 'Oh "good afternoon" is it? My my, ye're gettin awfy polute in yer auld age.'

P.R., *or* P.R.W. A familiar abbreviation for Paisley Road (West) a main thoroughfare of the South Side: 'If ye get onty the P.R. any bus'll take ye inty toon.'

Priestie, the A nickname for the Priesthill area in the South Side: 'She goat a cooncil flat in the Priestie efter her man goat aff his mark.'

Prosecutin Fiscal An alternative title for the Procurator Fiscal, commonly used amongst those who have cause to see his role in this light: 'Ah never done nuthin. Ah'm complainin tae the Prosecutin Fiscal aboot this.'

Provvy Cheque A slang term for a cheque issued by the Provident Personal Credit Ltd.: 'Evrubdy roon here gets the Christmas prezzies wi a Provvy Cheque.'
     This is a credit arrangement whereby someone borrows (at interest) a sum from this company, the funds being supplied as a cheque to be exchanged for goods at a shop displaying a sign that it accepts such cheques.

puddin A disparaging name applied to a plump person: 'Time you went back on a diet, ya big puddin.'

puff To **bother your puff** means to stir yourself, make an attempt: 'Ach, don't bother yer puff cookin. Ah wisny wantin any dinner, anyway.'

puff candy A type of confection of a hard, crumbly consistency that tends, as I recall, to stick to the teeth. The name is used, especially by schoolchildren, to characterise anything considered to be easily done: 'C'mon, just two more laps an that's us — it's pure puff candy tae the gemme kids.'
     Sometimes heard in a shortened form, as in: 'That's puff.'

puggy work Hard physical labour: 'It's awright fur you, sittin on yer arse giein oot orders, an it's me that's tae dae the puggy work.'

This perhaps comes from *puggy* in the sense of a railway steam engine formerly used for shunting.

punny *or* **punny eccy** School slang, used by both staff and pupils, for a punishment exercise, ie a written piece of work given to a child as punishment for some classroom crime: 'Ah canny come oot till Ah've finished this punny fur Aul Kipper.'

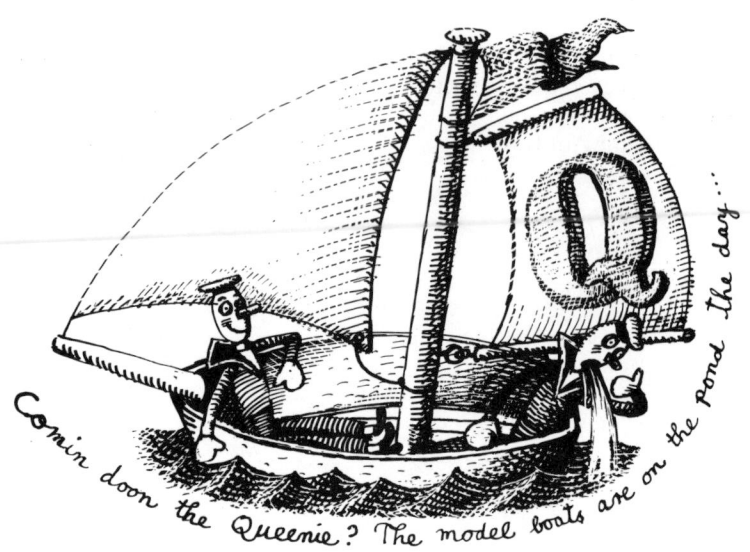

Comin doon the Queenie? The model boats are on the pond the day...

Queenie, the A familiar name for the Queens Park, a large public park on the South Side: 'Comin doon the Queenie? The model boats are on the pond the day.'

queued out A term used to describe any place or event that is very busy or crowded: 'We tried tae get inty the Odeon tae see that Rambo VII but when we seen it wis queued oot we jist came away.'

This is really a shortening of the fuller form **queued out the door** which, of course, is self-explanatory.

Rab Haw, the Glesga Glutton...

Rab Haw A name applied to any glutton or even to someone who merely has a big appetite: 'Ah went tae get merr soup but Rab Haw here had snaffled the lot.'

Rab Haw, or Robert Hall, was a real person, a vagrant who died in 1843 having become famous throughout the west of Scotland for his unparallelled eating capacity. His rapacious appetitie was often the subject of bets and it seems that those who backed Rab were invariably on to a good thing, as in one wager that involved his consuming a whole calf (except for the skin) that was served to him in the form of various pies. The story goes that having seen off the pies Rab was heard to enquire where was this calf he was meant to eat.

Another of his feats is preserved in the following rhyme:
Rab Haw, the Glesga Glutton,
  et ten loaves an a leg a mutton.

ranter A local word for a fool, especially a voluble one who talks a lot of rubbish: 'Whit mince is that ranter comin away wi noo?'

rats Someone who is very lively or can't sit still may be compared to a **bag of rats**: 'Can you no sit at peace till Ah get yer anorak on? Ye're like a bag a rats the day.'

rattle around A phrase meaning to be up and about, present and lively: 'Ah thought she'd huv the weans doon by noo but they're still rattlin aroon.'

red (or rid) rotten A phrase meaning very bad, absolute rubbish: 'That play he took us tae wis rid rotten. Nae actin in it, jist a few folk yatterin away aboot nuthin.'

remmy A schoolchildren's insulting name for someone considered stupid: 'Ye never fell fur that yin, did ye? Away ya remmy!'
   This comes from a shortening of remedial. In schools, remedial teaching is a type of special teaching given to children with learning difficulties. A child receiving such special attention is known as a remedial.

ribs Away an lie on yer ribs is another of these impolite phrases intended to tell someone that his presence is not desired: 'Whit d'ye mean "Where's ma coffee"? Ach, away an lie on yer ribs!'

ridiculous A slang term for helplessly drunk: 'The rest a them were still knockin it back good style but Ah wis ridiculous already.'

riggin Rigging, a football slang term for the goal-net: 'McStay took wan look up an bang! it's in the riggin.'

right Used locally to mean ready, fit, all set, and so on: 'Are ye right? Away we go then.'

ripped A slang word meaning under the influence of illicit drugs: 'Ye canny expect sense oot a sumdy that's ripped oot his nut hauf the time.'

roll about To laugh uproariously: 'Get um tae tell ye aboot gettin lost in Embra. We were rollin aboot when we heard it.'

rollie Short for a hand-rolled cigarette: 'Look at the size a the rollie he's gied me! Ye'd need a poultice tae get a draw oot it.'

rooked Completely out of money, skint: 'Another three days tae payday an here Ah'm rooked already.'

Rosie's Home A proverbial care facility for children, of a legendary strictness: 'The pair a ye are fur Rosie's Home if ye don't start behavin.'

rotten To be **caught rotten** is to be caught red-handed: 'Thought ye'd get away wi it, eh? Well ye were caught rotten so hell mend ye.'

Roukie, the A familiar name for Rouken Glen, an extensive public park on the South Side: 'Does the thirty-eight bus still take ye the length of the Roukie, son?'

Royal, the A common abbreviation for the Royal Infirmary: 'She was a Sister in the Royal before she came to Yorkhill.'

rubber ear To **throw** or **sling someone a rubber ear** means either to deliberately fail to hear someone, ignore him pointedly, or turn down someone who asks you out: 'What's the matter, son? She give ye a rubber ear, then?'
  I suppose the idea is that any remarks that fall on a rubber ear will bounce right back without making any impression.

Ruglonian A name applied to a native of Rutherglen, from the pronunciation of the place's name as Ruglen: 'Don't cry me a Glaswegian, sonny boy. Ah'm a born an bred Ruglonian.'

rummle A **rummle in the sheets** is a less than romantic way to describe a sexual encounter: 'Know whit the cheeky peasant says tae me? "Fancy a rummle in the sheets, doll?". Ah took ma haun aff his jaw.'

. blaw the simmit aff ye .

safe home A parting wish to someone leaving you late at night or having an especially long way to travel: 'See ye next Friday night then.' 'Aye, John, safe home now.'

Saltmarket The phrase **all the comforts of the Saltmarket** is a piece of irony meaning no comforts at all, no mod cons: 'That's some flat ye've landed noo, lassie. Talk aboot aw the comforts ae the Saltmarket!'
  This is a survival from the bad old days when this street running south from Glasgow Cross was infamous for its poverty. In its more recent stone-cleaned and refurbished state I'm sure the coiner of this phrase would have a job to recognise it.

Scabby Aggie An abusive name, particularly among schoolchildren, for any female considered unclean or simply unpopular: 'Don't tell us ye've tae sit next tae *that* Scabby Aggie?'

scabby touch, the Used in a children's game like tig. The difference is that it can begin spontaneously, as when someone is adjudged to have come into contact with something disgusting. He is then told he has the scabby touch and is obliged to touch someone else in order to pass on and free himself of the vile contagion: 'When Ah telt um Ah wis efter a refund he looked at us as if Ah'd gied um the scabby touch.'

scone A scone is another name for a man's flat bunnet: 'Wait till Ah stick ma scone on.'

Someone looking aggrieved or unhappy may be posed the unsympathetic question 'Who stole yer scone?'

scrappie A familiar term for a scrap-metal dealer: 'We'll nip doon the scrappie an see if we can pick up a spare wheel wi a good tyre on it.'

set-in bed A local term for a bed located in a bed-recess, still found in smaller tenement flats: 'Ah like a set-in bed, fur ye feel that cosy, daen't ye?'

seven-ender *or* **seven-sider** Nicknames for a fifty-pence piece: 'Gie's a couple a seven-enders fur the fag machine, wull ye?'

shadow Someone who is very argumentative may have it said of him that **he would fight with his shadow.**

sheathie A sheath-knife: 'He only joined the Scouts so he could get carryin a sheathie.'

Shaws, the A familiar name for the Pollokshaws area, on the south side: 'Oh him? He's wan a they queer folk a the Shaws.'

sheet To **put a sheet round** is to make a collection of money for someone who may be leaving a place of work, getting married, having a baby, and so forth: 'Did ye hear? Aul Miseryguts isny lettin us pit a sheet roon fur wee Sheila.'

To **put to (somebody's) sheet** is to make a contribution to such a collection: 'Ah've pit tae umpteen sheets this year. When is it gauny be ma turn?' The expression probably originated in the collection of cash in an actual bedsheet carried round in a neighbourhood.

Shields, the A familiar name for the Pollokshields area, on the south side: 'Is the Shields no a dry area?' 'If it is Ah know the guy that drank it dry.'

shirt button A nickname for a tweny-pence piece: 'Most a these parkin meters only take a shirt-button noo an ye've never got wan.'

shoogle-brain An idiot: 'OK, which one of you shoogle-brains wrote the charming message on the blackboard?'

The idea is that the person so stigmatised possesses a brain so small that it rattles when he shoogles his head.

shoot To shoot means to leave, depart, perhaps representing a shortened version of shoot the crow: 'Ach, Ah think Ah'll shoot early the day.'

To **shoot the boots off** someone is a vague mild threat of punishment, most often used by adults to children: 'If you manage to get that dress dirty before your auntie comes I'll shoot the boots off you.' There is a marked savour of the Wild West in this.

Something that is in a bad state of repair, falling apart, etc., may be described as being **shot to bits**: 'Time you had a new motor, hen. This yin's shot tae bits an it's due its M.O.T.'

shot Used in slang to mean any item, example, individual, etc. This is almost universally applicable. For example, a Highlandman might be referred to an 'an Angus Og shot', and a homosexual is a 'bent shot': 'Do you want the twenty-five or fifty pence size?' 'Gie's the ten-bob shot.'

This probably spread into everyday use from the specialised parlance of betting, where, for example, a horse starting at odds of 10-1 would be a 'ten-to-one shot.'

shots each A local expression meaning turn and turn about: 'There's only wan bike between yeez, so it's tae be shots each, OK?' 'The dirty ratbags were havin shots each at bootin um.'

shout To shout someone is to call him, alert him to something, such as the fact that it is time for him to get up: 'Ma Maw shouts us at hauf six.'; or that he has reached his destination: 'Shout us when we get to Queens Park please, driver.'

shuffle *or* **shuffle bettin** A slightly old-fashioned slang term for a betting shop: 'See if ye're gaun doon the shuffle, gauny stick this line on fur me?'

shunk *or* **shunkie** Slang words for a toilet: 'Ma eyebaws are floatin. Gauny mind ma pint tae Ah nick inty the shunk?'

It may be that there is a connection between this usage and the well-known manufacturer of lavatory fitments, Shanks.

sideyways As well as being a local version of sideways this is also used to refer to suicide: 'His faither committit sideyways — flung hissel ower the banister fae the tap flerr.'

signwriter An unemployed person who is fed up with having to tell people he is on the dole when asked what he does may adopt the smart answer of 'I'm a signwriter for the Social Security' ie I sign on.

simmit The Scots word for a vest appears in various proverbial phrases. For example, if something, especially an alcoholic drink, is regarded as very powerful you might be cautioned that **it wid blaw the simmit aff ye.**

If you are obliged to listen to a tale of woe from someone looking for sympathy, or you witness an event that is expected to move you, you might ironically say **it wid fair tear yer simmit.**

simple pimple A rhyming catchphrase used to describe anything considered easy: 'That's pure simple pimple. We'll be finished in no time.'

single A single is a loose cigarette, sold individually in a shop: 'Here Ah'm gaspin fur a drag an Ah huvny the price ae a tipped single.'

sittie-doon *or* **sittie-in** The opposite of carry-out (takeaway), these descriptions are applied to a meal eaten in a restaurant: 'Moan Ah'll take ye fur a sittie-doon Chinky. Ye get scunnered wi they carry-oots, don't ye?'

skelp it This can mean either of two things:
1. To have sex.
2. To work briskly at a job: 'We'll need tae skelp it if we've tae huv this finished the day.'

skinto A local variation of skint, ie broke, penniless: 'OK, wan merr can a ginger each an that's yer lot. Ye'll have yer aul granda skinto.'

Who knows why Glaswegians feel the need to add the Italianate ending?

skits A slang term for diarrhoea: 'That stuff wid gie ye the skits jist smellin it.'

This is a shortened form of skitters, which is more widely known.

skitterywinter A name applied to the last person to turn up for work in a factory, shipyard, office, etc. on Hogmanay (in some workplaces, also on Fair Friday). The unfortunate latecomer is greeted by his workmates banging loudly on any suitable surface. I believe the ceremony is no longer common but the term is still heard in wider contexts to mean anyone who is dilatory or lags behind: 'You no up yet, skitterywinter? How are you always last out yer pit?'

skooshed A slang word for dunk: 'He wis that skooshed ye couldny make oot a word he wis sayin.'

skunk's underpants A proverbial comparison for anything smelling unpleasantly: 'Goad, your breath's like a skunk's underpants this mornin.'

sky it To sky it means to make off rapidly, get off one's mark: 'We aw skied it when that big Alsatian came chargin oot.'
The expression can also be used as a warning: 'Sky it! Polis!'

skyhook One of these mythical things referred to in fool's errands on which new workers are sent: 'Away an see big George an tell um Ah said tae gie ye a skyhook.'
Also used in the phrase to **cast a skyhook**, meaning to take part in a pointless exercise: 'This is whit Ah call castin a skyhook, gaun tae this gemme wi nae tickets.'

slabberchops A name to call someone, especially a baby, who salivates or dribbles: 'Put a bib on wee Slabberchops or that Babygro'll be soaked in five minutes.'

sling-feed In popular mythology, this means to feed a child using a sling to fire food into its mouth. This is necessary because the child is so greedy that you can't spoon the stuff in fast enough and you risk him taking the hand off you in one gulp: 'Look at the wee man wirin inty that biryani. Ah bet his maw hud tae sling-feed um.'

slush A nickname for tea: 'We'll have a wee cup a slush if you'll stick the kettle on.'

smell In local usage to smell, apart from the usual meanings, can be used in the sense of giving a smell to, making a thing smell of something else: 'He sucks mints tae smell his breath but we aw know he's been at the bevvy.'

snakie A nickname for snakebite, a drink concocted of equal parts of cider and lager: 'If she's been on the snakies aw night it's nae wunner she's honkin her load.'

snapdragon A slang word for a toilet seat that proves to be badly balanced when lifted by a gentleman and falls down at an inconvenient moment: 'Ye can always tell when it's aw lassies in a flat — the lavvy seat's always a snapdragon.'

snapper A slang term for a child, probably shortened from *breidsnapper*: 'She's no really ma auntie, but Ah've always called her it since Ah wis a snapper.'

snotterybeak A disapproving name applied to someone with a runny nose: 'Wid sumdy gie Snotterybeak a len ae a hanky? That sniffin's drivin me up the waw.'
   Such a person may also have it said of him that **the snotters are trippin** (or **blindin**) **him.**

so A common local verbal phenomenon is the instant confirmation of what you have just said (a double positive?) by means of phrases beginning with so: 'That hat suits ye, so it does.' 'Ah'm gettin right fed up wi this, so Ah am.'

Social, the Short for Social Security, the D.H.S.S.: 'She got money fae the Social tae get shoes fur the weans.'

Society man, the Not someone who moves in refined circles, but a local term for a representative of the Co-operative Insurance Society who calls to collect periodical payments: 'Is this no the night fur the Society man?'

soldier A **good soldier** is a description given to someone who suffers illness or pain without excessive complaint. The opposite of this is, of course, a **bad soldier**: 'No gauny greet are ye, wee man? Naw, you're a good soldier, eh?'

Spam Valley A disparaging term for any suburban area of good housing and amenities in which live many people, especially younger couples, who have trouble affording it. Such people are said to have to economise to the extent of being obliged to include lots of Spam in their diet: 'Never thought Ah'd see a pair a tearaways like you movin inty Spam Valley.'

spanner A slang term for a can-opener: 'Dig out that spanner an Ah'll get the soup on.'

spin A lie or tall story: 'That's a pure spin he's giein us.'
   To spin is to kid or try to con someone: 'Ah'm no swallyin that wan. You're spinnin, pal.'

spinbin A slang word for a mental hospital: 'Her? Oh, she's in the spinbin. Ah'll never forget the night they took her away.'

split To batter someone: 'Ah'm gauny split this guy.' Sometimes expanded to **split someone's heid**: 'If he hears aboot this he's gauny split your heid, ya numshie.'

spur The phrase **take the spur** means to become annoyed, take offence: 'D'ye no see she's windin ye up? Don't take the spur an gie her the satisfaction.'

square tiff Most common in schools, this is another term for a square go, ie a stand-up fight, one to one, unarmed: 'Right you, that's you an me fur a square tiff in the ring, four o'clock.' 'In the ring' means that the two combatants are surrounded by a circle of spectators, usually chanting 'Ow! Ow! Ow!'

squid A gallus version of quid, that is, a pound sterling: 'Ah'm doon tae two squid an a haunfu a mince.'

S.S., the Not the Nazi organisation but the Social Security: 'Look for a shop that does S.S. estimates.'
A D.H.S.S. inspector is known as the **S.S. man.**

stakes Another term borrowed from the world of gambling, in this case from the titles of races, such as the *Queen Elizabeth II Stakes*. In the dialect this is used to give a descriptive name to any situation or circumstances: 'If Ah don't get some cash before the end a the month it'll be pure desperation stakes.'

stankie A children's game of marbles that makes use of the grille of a round stank (drain) as a playin surface on which the marbles sit neatly in the holes: 'We canny get playing stankie cause the gutter's choked.'

steakie A familiar term for a steak knife: 'The mad bastart went fur us wi a steakie.'

steam One rather picturesque way of saying to get drunk is **to get a good head of steam about you**: 'You had a good head a steam about ye when Ah bumped inty ye that night.' It gives an apt impression of a steam engine all stoked up and ready to chug along.

steamer A slang word for a drinking bout: 'When wis the last time you *wereny* on a steamer on a Friday night?'

steelies 1. A child's word for steel ball-bearings used as marbles: 'Ye canny play steelies against jorries. They jist stoat aw ower the place.'

2. A slang word for steel-toecapped protective working boots: 'Ah'd like tae get inty that toerag's heid wi ma steelies oan.'

stick A mild term of abuse, applicable to almost anyone: 'Did you scoff two caramel wafers, ya bad wee stick?' 'That's a carnaptious auld stick, that yin.'

stoat This word for bounce is also used in betting circles to mean win, as in: 'If this line stoats Ah'll get ye a doner kebab.'

stoat-the-baw A slang term for paedophile, from the comparison of patting a child's head to bouncing a ball: 'Leave ma wee brither alane, ya stupit-lookin stoat-the-baw, ye.'

stoatin An adjective used to describe any food item that is stale, has gone hard when it should be soft and would therefore probably bounce if dropped: 'If they scones are stoatin jist pap them in the bin.'

stoatybumper A slang term for anything excellent, being an amalgam of two other such words, *stoater* and *bumper*. 'Is this for me? Aw, ye're a wee stoatybumper, so ye are!'

storm damage A local version of 'a few slates missing', ie an implication that someone is not right in the head: 'Don't pay too much attention to what he says. There's a fair bit of storm damage there.'

Also used in adjectival form: 'C'moan oot a here. This guy's pure storm-damaged.'

story The question **what's the story** is commonly used to ask what is going on, what are the facts: 'What's the story wi you an this wee burd fae Possil?'

The related question 'what's *your* story?' has more hostile overtones and is equivalent to 'what are you playing at' or 'what could you possibly have to say that would be at all relevant': 'Hey, bawheid! Aye, you! What's your story, eh?'

The term **true story** is used to describe anything that you want someone else to believe: 'Away, you're havin us on.' 'Naw, true story, pal, honest.'

stove To **stove in** or **get stoved in** means to partake of something enthusiastically: 'Help yersels tae the champagne, lads, an get stoved inty they canapés.'

striped face A graphic description of a face that bears slash marks or scars: 'You wantin a striped face, pal? Well, shut it, then.'

student tobacco A slang term for marijuana, arising from the alleged fondness for it of those in higher education, although its consumption is hardly exclusive to them: 'The wee brother hardly ever takes a drink. He's more inty the student tobacco, ye know?'

stupit-lookin A local abusive adjective, particularly popular among those who prefer not to swear: 'Gaun, ya stupit-lookin daft big clown, ye.'

Suckie A nickname for Sauchiehall Street: 'How far up Suckie is that Third Eye Centre place?'

sunbeam A jocular form of address, often used ironically to someone looking less than cheerful: 'Are ye winnin, sunbeam?'

Sweaty Betty A legendary Glasgow female character troubled by excessive perspiration: 'See this heat? Look at the oxters a this dress . . . Sweaty Betty's no in it!'
This lady is often accompanied by her equally mythical pal Hairy Mary.

sweeties This, of course, is the Scots word for confectionery and it has several local uses. Someone who feels that he is underpaid in his job may complain of **working for sweeties.**
Similarly, low wages are often referred to as **sweetie-money:** 'Ye're workin fur sweetie-money in here. Ye'd be better aff on the broo.'
Someone who is very fond of sweeties can be labelled **sweetie-face:** 'Put the chocolates by before wee sweetie-face comes in.'

swimmies An abbreviated term for one's swimming gear: 'Don't forget yer swimmies the morra.'

swings **A shot on the swings** is a slang expression for the sexual act: 'Good weekend, was it? D'ye get a shot on the swings, aye?'

Time that wean wis walkin.
She's a ton weight.

taddie A local familiar name for the tadpole: 'Any jamjaurs, Maw? We're gaun fur taddies.'

talleyman A slang word for a moneylender or loanshark: 'Ah'm inty the talleyman fur a hunner.' Presumably the name comes from the idea of the moneylender keeping a tally of how much he is owed and by whom.

tan 1. **To tan something** is to use it up very quickly: 'We ferr tanned that hauf boatle'; or to work briskly at it: 'If we tan these last few orders we'll get away early the night.'
2. **To tan a house** is to burgle it: 'The polis says it's young boays that's tannin the hooses roon here.'

Tanics *or* **Tannies** Nicknames for the Botanic Gardens, in the West End: 'It wis a crackin day the day. Thae Tanics were full a punters sunbathin.'

tank Used in slang to mean, especially of money, your lot, all you have on you: 'Don't tell us that's yer tank? Here, Ah'll len ye a five-spot.'

tap To tap someone is to borrow money from him: 'See if ye can tap a couple a quid aff the aul boy.'
   A tap is a loan of money: 'Here's Big Peter; he's usually good for a tap.'

D

taste In a similar manner to *smell*, in dialect this is used to mean that a substance leaves a flavour of itself on something else: 'Ah canny go anythin garlicky. It tastes ma mouth for hours after it.' 'Don't leave yer milk out while Ah'm paintin or the paint'll taste it.'

team-handed A slang expression used when an individual has a crowd of friends (his 'team') with him: 'Aye, ye're feart tae show yer face roon here unless ye come team-handit, ya crapbag, ye.'

Teddy-bear Country CB enthusiasts' slang for the Ibrox area: 'Ah'm no parkin overnight on a Saturday in Teddy-bear country wi a green motor!'

The explanation, for those unable to work it out, is that the home ground of Glasgow Rangers F.C. is in Ibrox, and Teddy Bears is a nickname for this team.

Teenie **Teenie fae Troon** is a disparaging name applied to any female who presents a hoity-toity image or is much too fancily dressed for her surroundings: 'Wull ye look at Teeny fae Troon ower there . . . where dis she think she is at aw?'

Teenie Leek is an affectionate name applied to a female child: 'Come on, Teenie Leek, time you were in your bed.'

tell When a child means to inform a parent, teacher, etc. of another child's misdemeanour he may say: 'Ah'm tellin.' The unrepentant transgressor will immediately riposte: 'You're smellin.'

If someone is given a brusque reply to a question or statement he may say: 'That's me told (or telt).'

To be told means to take a telling, accept a warning: 'Ah've said he's tae chuck it time an time again but he won't be told.' Sometimes the words are used as a last warning; 'Now what did Ah say a minute ago? Be told!'

ten to two Someone who is splay-footed may be described as having **ten-to-two feet**, ie resembling the hands of a clock at this time.

this is me Not a redundant introduction of yourself but part of a description of your circumstances: 'This is me since yesterday, nuthin tae eat. 'Ah canny shift this cold at aw. This is me loaded fae last Tuesday.'

thorn A slang word, particularly in the building trade, for a nail: 'See's a handfu a thorns, will ye?'

Timothy Tight-arse *or* **Timothy T.A.** A disparaging title for someone who
  1. Has the backside hanging out of his trousers.
  2. Thinks he's gallus and isn't.

toad If you suspect someone of being economical with the truth you might call him a **lyin toad**, although I cannot see why the poor amphibian should be so slandered.

toley-poker A horribly vivid slang word for a drug-squad policeman, arising from the fact that they are often involved in intimate body-searches.

ton weight A term applied to anything, including people, considered to be very heavy: 'Time that wean wis walkin. She's a ton weight.'

toofty Pretentious, twee, or snobbish: 'Are the folk no kinna toofty up in Pollokshields?'

toon To go **doon the toon** is a slang phrase used to mean work as a prostitute, go on the streets: 'How'm Ah meant tae feed an dress these weans on ma own; go doon the toon or somethin?'

toss[1] **To toss** something is to throw it out, throw it in the bin: 'Well, if ye canny get it workin jist toss it.'

toss[2] A disparaging slang term, literally meaning a masturbator, but most often used simply to mean an idiot: 'Whit're you sayin, ya toss?'
  A variant form with the same meaning is **tossbag**: 'Tell that tossbag ae a mate a yours tae get lost.'

tosser To describe something as being **not worth a tosser** means that it is of very little value or it is in poor condition: 'Ah'm no worth a tosser since Ah've had this flu.'
  Not to give a tosser means you couldn't care less: 'Disny matter whit ye say, he couldny gie a tosser.'
  These expressions both derive from the penny coin used in the gambling game of pitch and toss, that was known as the tosser.

tote A slang name for the Department of Employment, the office where the unemployed go to sign on to claim Unemployment Benefit. For those who are unfamiliar with racing terminology, tote is a betting term, short for Totalizator, denoting a system of betting whereby, roughly speaking, winners receive a percentage of the total amount staked on a race: 'Sure Wednesday's your day for the tote?'

totties A woman whose figure lacks shape or who wears an ill-fitting dress may find herself compared to **a bag a totties tied in the middle.**

toytown money A contemptuous term for pound coins: 'Don't give us any of that toytown money. I want pound notes.'

trackie A local shortening of tracksuit: 'Da, Da, know whit Ah want fur ma Christmas? A Scotland trackie.'

traffic A phrase addressed to someone you want rid of, especially used among children, is **away an play in the traffic,** ie go and get knocked down by a motor vehicle.

Trannie A nickname for the Transcard, a kind of limited season ticket for local transport, lasting for varying periods and covering buses, trains, and Underground: 'Aw naw, driver, Ah've gone an left ma Trannie in ma ither jaiket.' 'Aye, that's whit they aw say. Aff!'

trebbal (pronounced treh-*bal*) A schoolkids' term meaning very good, excellent, but very often used in an ironic or sarcastic way to mean the opposite: 'What, merr homework? Aw, trebbal, miss!'
   This is a bizarre piece of language that I can only guess comes from a deliberate distortion of treble, used to mean treble good or something Orwellian like that.

tree If you want to imply that someone's ideas are not very sensible you might say that he's **just swung doon oot a cherry** (*or* **banana) tree.** Similarly, you might say **you're aff yer tree.**

trouble-the-hoose A title given to a young baby whose crying and urgent needs inevitably disturb the peace of the household: 'See's ower wee Trouble-the-hoose till her aul granda gets a shot of her.'

troubles Someone who is beset by difficulties may have it said of him that he doesn't **have his troubles to seek:** 'She's no got her troubles tae seek since she got mixed up wi that useless ticket.'

tuppence Two pence in pre-decimal money, but still in use in various popular idioms. A small child may be described as being **no the size a tuppence.**

No worth tuppence can mean that a thing is of no value, or, applied to people, that someone is completely exhausted: 'Ah'm no worth tuppence efter Ah've come up they stairs.'

turn A **turn** is a win at gambling, perhaps deriving from the punter's necessary faith that everyone must have a turn to be lucky: 'Ah see Joe's had a turn. Away an nip him for a blue job.'

Ye jist cannae be up tae um!

up In the field of gambling, to describe something as being up means that it has won: 'Maybe we'll have the coupon up this week.' 'That's me got a line up.'

The phrase **ye canny be up tae um** is said of someone, especially a mischievous child, whose behaviour is impossible to predict: 'Ah sent um inty the hoose cause he wis pullin up ma daffadils an when Ah went in he wis feedin the baby a dug biscuit . . . ye jist canny be up tae um!'

He used tae work in Pearson's in Vicky Road, feedin the parrot...

Vicky, the A familiar name for the Victoria Infirmary: 'She's got that much wrong with her she's got a season ticket for the Vicky.'

Vicky Road A familiar name for Victoria Road, a main business and shopping thoroughfare on the South Side: 'He used tae work in Pearson's in Vicky Road, feedin the parrot.'

Right intae the wid...

wacky baccy A slang term for marijuana: 'What're you gigglin at... been at the wacky baccy or somethin?'

Walk, the The name by which most people refer to the Orange Walk, held each year on the Saturday nearest to the twelfth of July: 'We were held up for ages with the Walk goin along the Paisley Road.'

To **break the Walk** is to cross the street in front of or through a gap in the main body of the parade, a practice that should carry a government health warning.

There are other minor Orange marches in the summer, before July, and these are known as **wee walks.**

wallies A collective term for a very small sum, especially poor wages: 'Ye get paid wallies in that place.

wally heid Someone who is described as having a **wally heid** is considered simple-minded, not right in the head.

Similarly, to call someone **a wally-heid** means you think he is a simpleton.

wally waw Literally porcelain wall, this means a gents' urinal of the kind consisting of one complete porcelain receptacle running the length of a wall: 'Ach well, Ah'll away an staun at the wally waw.'

washers Pronounced to rhyme with rashers, this is a disparaging term for small change: 'Got change of a pound? Two fifties, though, not a load a washers.'

washin (rhymes with passion) Someone who is depressed, listless, inanimate, may be told he is **hingin aboot like a wet washin.**

watterheid A slang term for a person regarded as being not quite right in the head, perhaps a reference to water on the brain: 'Hey, watterheid! Whit're you meant to be daein?'

well got A local variant of well in, being on good terms with: 'Aye, he gets aw the overtime he wants cause he's well got wi that supervisor.'

wellied To **get wellied in** means the same as get stuck in, that is, to set about something vigorously: 'What's up wi ma dinner that naebdy's wantin seconds? Just get wellied in there.'

West-Endie An inhabitant of Glasgow's West End, an area roughly west of Charing Cross, north of Argyle Street, south of Maryhill Road, and shading away westwards to the far suburbs. This is its geography, but some would say it is more a state of mind. It is the famous home of students (real and pretend ones), artists (ditto), and fashionables. The fuller form of the term, **trendy West-Endie** gives an idea of how this subculture is viewed in other parts of the city. Also used as an adjective: 'Ah fancy nippin doon wan a they trendy West-Endie pubs in Byres Road fur a wee change.'

Western, the To say that someone is in the Western is not to imply a role in a cowboy film but that he is a patient in the Western Infirmary.

whack The phrase **not the full whack** means incomplete, not up to scratch, below par: 'Are you OK? You're not lookin the full whack today at all.'

Whatevery's A local nickname for any branch of What Every One Wants, a chain of lower-price clothes shops: 'She says she got the exact same coat at Whatevery's fur hauf the price.'

whit This Scots form of 'what' appears in a local formula for emphatically denying a question the speaker himself has rhetorically asked: 'An wid he listen tae whit Ah wis tellin um? Would he whit!' This is obviously euphemistic for something stronger.

whitey *or* **white-oot** To take a whitey or white-oot means to suddenly turn pale because of feeling sick: 'See that boay takin a whitey? Get him oot inty the close away fae ma good carpet.'

wick A wick is an annoying or bad-natured person: 'Leave yer wee brither alane, ya wee wick, ye.'

wid A local variant of wood. Someone who has had a very short haircut may have it described as being right inty the wid.

wide The phrase to make someone wide means to let someone know some useful information, put him wise to the facts: 'Ah knew this wis gauny happen. Big Dan made us wide tae it the other night.'
A wide member is a flyman (see wido).

wido A slang term for a rogue, criminal, or flyman: 'The only folk that drink in here are neds, chancers, hardmen, an widos. Whit wan are you?'
This derives from the common slang use of wide, as in wide boy, meaning smart, fly, not completely honest.

wiggie An unkind name to call someone wearing an obvious hairpiece: 'D'ye think the Heidie knows the weans call him Aul Wiggie?'

Wine City A disparaging nickname, most common among CB enthusiasts, for the Greenock/Port Glasgow conurbation, deriving from the Glaswegian's belief that the natives thereof are great drinkers of cheap strong wine; a case, perhaps, of the pot calling the kettle black?

wineshop A slang term for a pub that specialises in selling cheap fortified wine by the glass: 'Naw, we don't stock that in here. It's a wine shop you're wantin, aul yin, no a wine bar.'

wing nut A nickname for anyone with ears that stick out: 'Here Wing Nut comin. He's like a car wi its doors opened.'

wired The phrase wired up but no plugged in is applied to anyone considered a bit simple, not all there: 'Ach, just never mind whit the boay tells ye. He's no the full shillin, if ye get whit Ah mean, wired up but no plugged in, ye know?'

Wired to the moon is a picturesque description of someone considered slightly mad, abnormally energetic: 'She's wired tae the moon, her. Ye canny keep up wi her.'

Woodbine The well-known proprietary brand of cigarette has a proverbial function. Something that is useless, out of order, may have it said of it: 'That's as much use as a wet Woodbine.' Similarly, something that is nonsensical or stupid can be described as making 'as much sense as a wet Woodbine.'

work on To work on means to work beyond your normal hours, especially on overtime: 'Ye comin up the road?' 'Naw, Ah'm workin on the night.'

worky up In children's talk this means to get your swing going from a standing start to the speed and height of arc desired: 'You sit on the swing next to me an I'll show ye how to worky up.'

wrap it up *or* **in** To desist, stop doing something: 'If Ah don't hit the jackpot this time Ah'm fur wrappin it up.'

Wrap it! is a menacing indication to someone that he should stop what he is doing, especially in the sense of 'shut up'.

X, Y &

·Big zeds.

yelp A child that is continually whingeing or being cheeky: 'Aye, an that lassie a theirs is a right wee yelp an aw.'

zed To **have a few zeds** and **stack up some zeds** are slang expressions for having a sleep. **Big zeds** means a long deep sleep, as opposed to a nap: 'Ah'm definitely needin big zeds the night. Ma eyes are hingin oot ma heid.'

The origin of all this is children's comics which conventionally show that someone is asleep by inserting a string of these letters in the picture.

RHYMING SLANG

One of the factors that make rhyming slang unintelligible to the uninitiated is that in an example that consists of two words the second component (which provides the rhyme) is often omitted. For this reason, I list my items in alphabetical order according to the first word. Thus, a reader may find the meaning of an expression suspected of being rhyming slang even if he only has the first part in mind.

Abraham (or Abie) Lincoln Stinkin: 'Your feet are Abraham Lincoln.'

acme wringers Fingers. The fact that this rhymes is an illustration of the local pronunciation of fingers. An Acme Wringer I assume to be a proprietary brand of clothes wringer.

Arthur Lowe No, ie a negative answer: 'Fancy another?' 'Ah widny say Arthur.' The late Arthur Lowe was, of course, a household name, particularly in the 1970s, as star of such TV comedy series as *Dad's Army*.

Bayne and Ducket A bucket, using the name of a well-known chain of shoe shops. Sometimes used as an exclamation, suggesting something a good deal stronger.

Bengal Lancer A chancer: 'Whit's that big Bengal sayin noo?'

Bob Hope Dope, ie marijuana: 'Fancy a blast a the old Bob?'

breid an watter Patter: 'He's the wee boy fur the breid an watter. Wait tae ye hear um.'

Carolina China, meaning a friend. This is an example of one piece of rhyming slang standing for another, as *china* itself is also rhyming slang (china plate = mate).

Chic Murray The late and much lamented droll comedian's name is taken in vain for a curry: 'Ah wish Ah'd went straight hame efter the pub instead a gaun fur that Chic!'

Cowdenbeath Teeth: 'Ah'll jist run the brush roon the aul Cowdenbeath then Ah'm inty ma scratcher.'

cream cookie A bookie, including his premises or betting shop: 'Away doon the cream cookie an lift whit's lyin fur this line.'

Crossmyloof Poof, ie male homosexual. Crossmyloof is an area of the South Side, until recently famous for its skating rink.

deedle doddle Model, ie Model Lodging House, a cheap hostel for the homeless: 'You're gaun about like somethin out the deedle doddle.'

dirty beast A priest.

disco dancer A chancer: 'He's a bit ae a disco dancer that pal a yours, eh no?'

dolly dimple Simple, in the sense of stupid: 'Ye'll need tae excuse her ... she's a wee bit dolly.'

Donald Pears (after a well-known singer) Ears.

Duke of Argylls Piles, that is, haemorrhoids: 'You'll get the Duke ae Argylls if ye sit on that cold waw much longer.'

Duke of Montrose Nose.

Easter egg Beg, as in **on the Easter egg**, begging for money: 'Never mind comin roon here on the Easter egg, ya aul moocher, ye.'

Eglinton Toll Arsehole: 'Are you gauny get aff yer Eglinton an make a move?'

Elsie Tanner A wanner, ie a single complete example of something: 'Whit d'ye hink? Anither coat a emulsion on the ceilin or lee it wi an Elsie Tanner?'
   This derives from the name of former well-known character in the TV soap-opera *Coronation Street*.

everlastin joob-joob A tube, ie the slang word for an idiot: 'Look at the mess ye're makin, ya everlastin joob-joob.'
   The term literally means a kind of long-lasting sucking sweetie.

Garngad (an area in the north-east of the city) Bad: 'We've no done too Garngad the day.' This, of course, is dependent on the local pronunciation which accents the second syllable.

gas-cookered Snookered, ie thwarted, prevented from getting something done: 'If that last nut'll no shift we'll be gas-cookered.'

gasket jint (jint being the local pronunciation of joint, on the model of jiner, joiner) A pint, usually of beer: 'Moan we'll nick oot fur a couple a gaskets.'

Gene Tunney Money. This one shows its age when you know that Gene Tunney was an American boxer who was world heavyweght champion 1926-28.

George Melly Belly: 'Check the George Melly he's got on him now.' George Melly is famous for many talents, particularly jazz singing and writing, as well as for flamboyant dress, but not for slimness.

ham sandwich Language. This only works if you remember that the second part is pronounced sangwidge: 'Just keep the ham sangwidge respectable in front a ma aul dear, eh?'

Harry Wraggs Jags, which is, of course, a nickname for Partick Thistle F.C.: 'We're The Jags, Harry Wraggs!'
The individual whose name is borrowed here was a famous racing jockey and trainer in the 1930s.

haw maw In the singular this can mean a saw: 'Emdy see wherr Ah left the big haw maw?'. In the plural it means baws, ie testicles: 'Ooyah, right in the haw maws!' 'Ye've made a right haw maws a this.'
The expression **haw maw** itself is a cry to attract the attention of one's mother.

hey diddle diddle Fiddle, in the sense of a swindle: 'He was caught at the hey diddle diddle with the books.'

holy ghost The coast: 'Fancy a wee run doon the holy ghost if it's nice the morra?'

hot peas Knees.

Jack an Jill The Pill: 'She's wantin tae come aff the jack.'

Jack dash A slash, ie urination: 'Just let us have a jack dash then we're off.'

jaggy nettle Kettle: 'Stick the jaggy on for a coffee.'

jam tart Fart: 'Did you just jam there?' 'Ye wanty've heard the jam tarts he wis lettin aff.'

Jeely jar Car: 'Is this the new jeely jar, eh?'

Jock Mackay A pie: 'Ah hud a couple a Jock Mackays fur ma tea.' This mythical person also turns up in an expression said as a sigh: 'Och aye, Jock Mackay.'

Joe Baxi A taxi: 'Never mind the motor. We'll dive inty a Joe Baxi.'

Joe the toff Off, ie away, gone, on one's way: 'Right, that's me Joe the toff. Cheerybyes!'

Kenneth Mackellar A cellar.

Legal Aid Lemonade: 'A wee splash a the Legal Aid in wan a they haufs, young yin.'

lemon curd Burd (bird), ie a girlfriend: 'Canny make it the night. It's the lemon curd's birthday.'

Lilian Gish I'm sure the famous star actress whose career began with Hollywood silent movies would not be amused to learn that her name is rhyming slang for pish. Similarly, **Lilian Gished** means drunk.

love an romancin Dancin: 'Ma folks are away tae the love an romancin at The Plaza.'

Macnamara A barra, ie barrow: 'Gie us a haun tae load these bricks inty the macnamara, wull ye?'

merry laird Beard (in local pronunciation, baird or berrd): 'Ah see ye've taken aff the merry laird.'

Mickey Mouse Grouse, ie a measure of the famous proprietary brand of whisky: 'A Mick Jagger an a Mickey mouse, barman.'

Mickey Rooney A loony: 'It's no joke stayin through the waw fae a Mickey Rooney lik that.'

Mr Happy A nappy: 'It's definitely your turn to change the wee guy's Mr Happy.'
Mr Happy is, of course, the smiling symbol of the 'Glasgow's Miles Better' campaign.

mountain goat A coat: 'Ah'm pittin oan ma mountain goat, case it gets hillbilly later oan.'

Paddy McGuire A fire: 'Sling another shovel on the Paddy McGuire while ye're up.'
I take this to be in reference to a supposedly typical Irish name rather than to any particular individual.

pan breid Deid, ie dead: 'Ye never telt us yer dug wis pan breid.'

paraffin ile (ile being a local pronunciation of oil) Style: 'Ye've really put on the paraffin the night, hen.'

Parkheid smiddies Diddies, ie a woman's breasts. This comes from a famous forge in Parkhead, in the city's East End.

Pat an Mick Sick: 'He's huvin a couple a days aff oan the Pat an Mick.'

pot of glue A clue: 'He hasny got a pot, stumer that he is.'

raspberry ripples Nipples. Often shortened to **rasps**: 'Can you see ma rasps through this blouse?'

rinky dinky dinky A Chinky, ie a Chinese meal: 'Whit're ye fur the night? A rinky dinky dinky or a Chic Murray?'

rooty-ma-toot Suit: 'Should Ah wear ma rooty-ma-toot fur this do?'
I think this expression is a kind of onomatopoeic representation of the sound of a bugle or trumpet, which might suggest that the term's origin was during the last war.

Scotland the brave A wave (of the hand), often shortened to **Scotland**: 'There's wee Mick ower the road giein us a Scotland.'

single fish Pish: 'Ah'm away fur a single fish.' 'Well, get us a pie supper.'

skin diver *or* **sky diver** A fiver, ie a five-pound note: 'Emdy got change of a skin diver?'

song an dancer A chancer: 'Ah hear the new boyfriend's a bit of a song an dancer.' What I like about this one is the particular aptness of its image of an entertainer or showbiz smoothie.

south of the border 1. Out of order, in the sense of being not quite right, not the done thing in terms of behaviour: 'Here, is that no a wee bit south of the border, whit he's sayin?'
 2. Order, as in: 'A wee bit a south fur the singer.' This of course refers to Mexico, not England, and is one of many examples of the Glaswegian love for and identification with the Western Movie.

tackety bits (ie hobnailed boots) Tits. Often shortened to **tacketies**: 'That's a fine perr a tacketies on that wee thing.'

taury (ie tarry) **rope** The Pope: 'When wis it the aul taury rope wis at Bellahouston Park?'

teedle-ee A pee, ie urination: 'He'll no be long. He's just away for a teedle-ee.'
 I would take this as coming from deedling, that is singing meaningless words in imitation of music played by a band.

Texas Ranger Danger. Sometimes heard in the form of an abbreviation: 'Ye're no gaun already?' 'No T.R. Ah'm just gettin warmed up noo.'

Tommy Trotter Snotter: 'Ye've a wee Tommy Trotter at your nose.'
 I don't know if this refers to a real person, but if so, he must have been fairly unpleasant to be so commemorated.

tin flute A suit: 'Must be daein awright fur hissel. Goes tae work in a tin flute an aw that.'

Toryglental Mental, ie crazy. I wonder what the residents of Toryglen did to merit this?

Rhyming slang for first names

A certain amount of this exists, although perhaps not as widespread as the bulk of ordinary rhyming slang. I include it for interest's sake and list below as many examples as I have come across, fully aware, of course, that there is bound to be more out there.

Alabammy Sammy.

Chanty Po Joe. This of course means a chamber pot, a somewhat unflattering label to be stuck with.

Clydebank an Kilbooie Shooey, ie Hugh.

Erskine Ferry
Finnieston } All stand for Merry, a local pronunciation of Mary.
Govan Ferry

Esso Blue Hugh.

Peas an Barley Charlie.

Puff Candy Andy.

Scapa Flow Joe.

Sparkin Plug Shug, ie Hugh.

Steak an Kidney Sidney.

Scrappies' rhyming slang

Again this is in limited use. My excuse for including it is that the few examples I have had drawn to my attention are both inventive and amusing. I am sure that other trades or occupations must have similar specialist rhyming slang but I have not come across this . . . yet.

Dennistoun Palais Aluminium (rhymes when shortenend to ally).

Midnight Mass Brass.

Missin Link Zinc.

Pottit heid Leid, ie lead.

PHRASES AND SAYINGS

a blind man running for a bus wouldn't notice
Said jocularly of something that is considered good enough to pass a cursory inspection, having imperfections slight enough to make little real difference.

Ah could eat a farmer's arse through a hedge
I am so hungry that not only would I tackle a less-than-appetising meal but I would let no difficulty in getting at it prevent me.

Ah could eat a scabby-heidit wean
I am so hungry that not only am I prepared to turn cannibal but I would not be too finicky about the choice of dish.

Ah could sleep on the edge ae a razor
I am exhausted, asleep on my feet: 'Ah don't gie a toss where Ah get the heid doon the night cause Ah could sleep on the edge ae a razor.'

Ah hate tae hear burds fartin that's got nae arse
A highly poetic excursion through the realms of ornithology, the parameters of human hearing, and surrealism, that all boils down to saying, I can't stand a braggart.

Ah never boil ma cabbages twice
I have no intention of repeating myself.

Ah wish ye health tae wear it
A conventional remark addressed to anyone who has recently obtained some new item of clothing.

Ah wouldny go oot wi um if he fartit ten-bob notes
He's not my type. The feat required to win the speaker's affections became even more unlikely with the introduction of decimal currency.

Ah'm no fur havin it
I am not in favour of this; I will not put up with this: 'He's wantin tae lower

the ceilin in the livin room but Ah'm no fur havin it. The place is wee enough already.'

Ah've hud fruit aff your barra before
Once bitten, twice shy; you don't catch me out a second time.

as Irish as the pigs of Docherty
Unmistakably a product of the Emerald Isle: 'Imagine him thinkin ma Mammy wis a Tally, an her as Irish as the pigs a Docherty.' Docherty I can see as being pretty Irish, but I'm not at all sure about how the nationality of his swine could be so incontrovertibly established as to function as a yardstick.

as rare as a Coatbridge Orangeman
A phrase describing something considered highly unusual: 'Chances of overtime in this place are aboot as rare as a Coatbridge Orangeman.' I need hardly explain that the population of Coatbridge is reputed to be overwhelmingly Roman Catholic in religious persuasion.

breath like a burst lavvy
A withering description of the breath of a halitosis sufferer or of someone merely exhibiting one of the antisocial side-effects of a hangover.

by the way
This little phrase is notorious for turning up in every conceivable context, whether it belongs there or not. Like the similar tack-on expression **an that**, it has become a mere verbal space-filler or oral lubricant helping actual relevant words to issue in a reasonably fluid manner. I fully expect one day to hear someone who is asked his name to reply: 'Jimmy, by the way.'

come in if your feet's clean
A jocularly irreverent invitation to enter someone's home.

could start a fight in an empty house
Said of someone who is naturally belligerent or loves an argument for its own sake: 'It wisny ma Robert's fault. That boay a yours could start a fight in an empty hoose.'

couldny hear him behind a caur ticket
A disparaging remark describing anyone who is either very small in

stature or so quiet as to be insignificant. A caur, of course, is not a motor car but a tramcar, something not seen on Glasgow streets for over twenty years, yet this phrase came to my attention via a secondary school pupil. This is another example of how a language preserves a term that is useful or memorably vivid.

couldny tackle a fish supper

Said of a footballer whose challenges are seen to lack bite, or more generally of anyone considered weak.

did ye faw an break yer watch?

An ironic, ostensibly sympathetic, enquiry to a child who has fallen and, although obviously unhurt, is making a fuss. Watch, in this case, is a euphemism for bottom.

doesn't know if it's New Year or New York

Said of anyone who is obviously not thinking clearly, whether because of being none too clever to begin with, or feeling the effects of an intoxicant or a shock of some kind: 'They don't know if it's New Year or New York, hauf a these kids leavin school the noo.'

don't give us it

Don't expect me to believe that: 'Look, ye were seen winchin in the bus shelter, so don't give us it ye wereny oot last night.'

don't give us the beef

Stop moaning or complaining. Another version of this is **don't give us the bully.**

gaun yersel Morton!

A cry meant to encourage any underdog. Morton are, of course, a football side from Greenock who, at least in recent years, are not expected by anyone other than partisan diehards to win anything.

get a kick of the ball

To be given an opportunity, have a chance to make your contribution. Another example of terminology from the national obsession, football, crossing over into everyday language: 'Aye, it'll be a different story when Labour get a kick of the ball.'

has emdy got a stick tae hit us wi?

An ironic phrase said by someone who is being verbally chastised and wishes to make the point that enough is enough.

have you been singin?

A jocular question asked of anyone who is carrying such a lot of small change that he is suspected of busking in the street: 'Look at aw the smash he's giein us. Have ye been singin or have ye done the meter?'

hing aboot like a bad smell

To loiter around in an irritating manner: 'Gauny go oot fur a walk or somethin instead a hingin aboot the hoose lik a bad smell?'

hold your water

To keep a secret; most often found in the negative: 'It wis meant tae be a surprise but aul Motor-mouth here couldny hold his water.'

honey from the dunny, a

A dunny is of course a basement or cellar in a tenement building. This expression refers to any woman who has come from a rough background and, although she may try to maintain a veneer of sophistication, constantly gives herself away: 'The manageress stays in Newton Mearns but Ah know a honey frae the dunny when Ah see wan.'

if Ah don't see ye aboot Ah'll see ya a sanny

A parting witticism, playing on aboot as a boot. A sanny is a sandshoe. There is also a suggestion of the local use of see to mean pass or give, as in 'see us they boots.'

if he was chocolate he would eat himself

A typically ego-destroying remark aimed at anyone who has a high opinion of his own worth.

if it's for ye it'll no go by ye

A fatalistic catchphrase meaning that what will be will be, that the events of life are somehow predestined and cannot be avoided by personal initiative. It tends to be used when something unfortunate occurs rather than in reference to a piece of good luck.

it wasn't the cough that carried him off, but the coffin they carried him off in

A jocular catch-phrase uttered when someone has a bad cough, not really meaning anything beyond a play on words.

it would put a beard on ye *or* it would put years on ye

Said of something that is very tedious or long and drawn-out. Each is an eminently down-to-earth way of putting over the idea that time seems to elongate when you are bored and you are made to feel as if a much longer time has elapsed than the real time taken: 'Goany turn it tae STV? It wid pit a beard on ye, you an yer snooker!'

it's nae loss whit a freen gets

A conventional remark made by anyone who has given something to a friend. It is intended to deflect modestly any praise offered for the act of generosity.

let the bull see the coo

(bull pronounced like dull) A phrase used by someone who feels he has the necessary expertise for a given situation and wants a clear view of the problem: 'Oot ma road, yous. Let the bull see the coo till Ah get this sortit.' A similar phrase is **let the dug see the hare.**

like something that fell off a flitting

Literally, like something lost in the course of a removal, this disparaging phrase is used to describe anyone who is dishevelled or looks the worse for wear: 'Ye're lik somethin that fell aff a flittin the day. Has yer maw pawned the iron?'

like two plums in a wet paper bag

An appreciative description made by a male as he views an attractive female posterior. A variation on this which is perhaps not quite so praiseful is **like two puppies fightin under a blanket.**

looks like he's ready for a clap wi a spade

A rather callous remark made about someone who has the appearance of being not long for this world, having one foot in the grave, and so on.

Madras in evening, mad arse in morning

A smart little play on words usually delivered as a 'wise old saying', intended as a salutary warning against eating a curry that is hotter than you can handle.

mouth like a pocketful a douts

An insightful assessment of one of the unpleasant after-effects of a heavy drinking session, especially on someone who also smokes: 'Ah woke up on the carpet wi a mooth lik a pocketful a douts an a heid lik a sterrheid.'

Another version of this is **a mouth like a badger's arse.** I don't know why badgers should be regarded as particularly unpleasant in this area.

mouth like a row of condemned buildings

Said of anyone who has irregular or broken and stained teeth. Also heard in the form **teeth like a row of condemned houses.**

my name is Gough and I am off

A remark made by someone who is about to depart, its poetry almost qualifying it as rhyming slang. Interestingly enough, I have found no examples of people saying that their names were anything else with a suitable rhyme.

nose running like a burn

A graphic description of one of the symptoms of a streaming head cold: 'This cold's gauny be the death a me. Ma nose's runnin lika burn an ma heid's loupin.'

refuse nothin but blows

To accept anything and everything that is going: 'Well, if ye're no wantin it gie it tae me. Ye know Ah refuse nothin but blows.'

run round the table and a kick at the cat, a

If a harassed mother is preparing a meal and is continually interrupted by children asking 'what's for my tea?' and so on, she might reply with this phrase, which means 'nothing at all.'

take the bad look off

To give a necessary improvement to the appearance of something: 'Ye'd think they wid gie their front door a lick a paint tae take the bad look aff it.' 'When Ah went in evrubdy wis up dancin except they two, sittin at a table full a drinks, an wee Boaby says "C'moan sit doon here an take the bad look aff us."'

that'll do me till Ah get somethin tae eat

Jocular remark made by someone who has just consumed an enormous snack or who has eaten heartily and makes a joke of not being satisfied.

there's a smell a clay aff him

Said, somewhat ghoulishly, of anyone who looks ill and may be considered unlikely to live much longer: 'Did ye clock aul Morrison at the purvey? There's a smell a clay aff him awright.'

there's ma hand up tae God

An oath made to convince someone that you are telling the truth, often accompanied by physically holding up your right palm and placing the left, if free, over your heart. Often shortened to **hand tae God**: 'Ah'm tellin ye, hand tae God, no a word ae a lie.'

there's no two pun a her hingin the right way

She is rather oddly-shaped.

they're flyin low tonight

A code phrase used by one man to another to warn him that the zip of his fly is down.

thinks he's big but a wee coat fits him

A disparaging assessment of anyone who has an inflated opinion of himself, an example of a pronounced strain in Glasgow speech and attitudes: that of making sure everyone is cut down to size.

toffs are careless

An observation made when someone is seen to be spending a lot of money: 'D'ye hear whit they rushed um fur that leather jaikit? Aye, it's well seen toffs are careless.'

The phrase is often used ironically when only insignificant sums are involved: 'Never mind the two pence change, son. Toffs are careless, ye know.'

walk up and down till you're fed up

A remark intended to discourage someone from complaining continually about being hungry.

wan singer, wan song

Popularised by Billy Connolly, this catch-phrase is supposedly shouted in a pub or club, etc. when someone is trying to sing and others insist on joining in with unharmonious effect. In everyday language it can also be heard as a call for order when there is a confused debate going on: 'Hey yous, wan singer, wan song, eh? Let the boay speak his piece.'

what a face tae foley a baun

A remark made to a crying child, implying I suppose, that only happy smiling faces should be seen following a band.

would drink it through a shitey cloot

A condemnatory phrase stigmatising someone as being so enamoured of strong drink that he will let no horror bar him from it: 'See him? See whisky? He wid drink it through a shitey cloot, so he wid.'

wouldny be held nor tied

A descriptive phrase used in reference to anyone who is extremely agitated, angry, or impatient: 'Ah wis late wi the wee soul's twelve o'clock feed. By the time he got his bottle he wouldny be held nor tied.'

wouldny be me

A stock assessment of a situation showing the speaker's disinclination to act similarly: 'Whit? Marry a guy that's got weans already? It wouldny be me, pal.'

wouldny gie ye . . .

These words appear as the overture to quite a range of phrases stigmatising meanness. I have included as many as I can gather but there is sure to be more.

> he wouldny gie ye a fright on a dark night
> he wouldny gie ye a spear if he wis a Zulu
> he wouldny gie ye daylight in a dark corner
> he wouldny gie ye the itch
> he wouldny gie a blind sparra a worm

wouldny make a back for a waistcoat

Said of someone who is considered very small or puny: 'The size ae um, tryin tae jine the polis! He widny make a back fur a waistcoat.'

wouldny walk the length of himself

A phrase used to condemn someone as bone-lazy: 'He wouldny walk the length of himself since he got that motor an now look at the beef he's carryin.'

you can't fatten a thoroughbred

A superior comment made by someone who is naturally slim and claims it is difficult for him to put on weight: 'It's awright fur you, you can eat whit ye like.' 'Well, ye canny fatten a thoroughbred, ye know.'

your pub's open

Another disguised way in which one man tells another that his fly is open.

CHEEK

Glaswegians are renowned for giving out cheek, at all ages and levels of society. This section may be treated by the stranger or incomer as a warning of what to expect if you leave yourself open with an injudicious conversational gambit. It should also be borne in mind that in conversation between people who know each other well the grossest insults and most ego-savaging observations may be exchanged without anyone taking offence, but you should be sure of your reception before you employ any of the following.

Ah don't know . . . the ticket's fell aff

A response on being asked belligerently 'What are you looking at?' The insult is in comparing the person involved to an item in a shop window or a museum exhibit.

Ah wouldny pull it fur a pension

An obscene jibe from a female to a male.

Ah've seen merr meat on a butcher's pencil

A male crack at a slim female; the kind of thing shouted from a building site at unfortunate passing women. Other variants of this are:

Ah've seen merr meat on a jockey's whip

Ah've seen merr meat on a well-chowed chicken bone

can you see better now?

A pseudo-solicitous question asked of someone who has just returned from a much-needed visit to the toilet.

d'ye want a photie?

A belligerent question addressed to anyone the speaker considers to have been staring at him.

d'ye want me tae scratch yer heid?

A mocking enquiry of someone who is bragging, the implication being that his head is now so big that he can't quite reach to scratch it himself.

dogs always smell their own dirt first

Said to someone who complains of a bad smell, particularly if insinuating that a person in the company is responsible for it.

is that your hair ye're wearin?

An insolent question addressed to someone you think has been guilty of a silly action, meaning are you right in the head? The literal significance of this is somewhat opaque, perhaps implying that you might not have the right head on your shoulders, or maybe that you are sporting a clown's wig.

must have been a lie

The standard retort made to anyone who says he has forgotten what he was going to say.

not since Jean Harlow died

A witty crack made by a female in reply to an innocent request of 'Have you got a match?' Presumably, if you are male you might substitute Errol Flynn, Clark Gable, etc.

put her on a piece an eat her

A terribly unromantic suggestion to be shouted at a kissing couple, demonstrating the local contempt and distrust for public displays of passion where football or inebriation are not involved.

so dae Ah, sodie watter

A contemptuous remark made to a person whose sole contribution to a conversation is merely saying 'so dae Ah' to any other individual's statement.

that's a fine perr a legs, hen . . . any finer an they'd break

An insolent male comment to a female whose legs are considered too thin.

what d'ye want me tae dae? Burst oot in fairy lights?

Said by someone refusing to be as excited or impressed as the person talking thinks he should be.

yer hair's lovely . . . been tyin knots in it?

An insensitive comment passed on a female's new hairstyle.

yer maw's a big man

A would-be withering insult exchanged between children.

your nose is too near your arse

An imputation of personal uncleanliness inflicted upon someone foolish enough to say that he detects an unpleasant odour.